Bati

Lyqa Planet Lovers

Nikki Clarke

This is a work of fiction. Names, characters, businesses, places, events and incidents are either the products of the author's imagination or used in a fictitious manner. Any resemblance to actual persons, living or dead, or actual events is purely coincidental.

Cover Art: L.M. Byfield

To my first reader, Hayyah. I know Ah'dan is your favorite, and he's coming soon.

(*ba ta bum*)

Note from Nikki

This is the second story in the Lyqa series. While you don't necessarily have to read the first one, there are some spoilers throughout, so you may want to read Kwarq first. A little more Lyqa never hurts.

Nikki

Prologue

BATI

"Yes, can I help you?"

The woman smiles warmly behind the wire gate blocking my entrance into her home. She looks like Amina. She's probably old enough to be my own mother, yet she appears many years younger than her age. Her skin is tight and smooth. The amber flesh looks bright and vibrant. Twisted strands of grey-threaded hair spike about her head. Her round, plump face and wide, heavily lidded eyes are just like her daughter's. At the moment, they're cautious. My tall frame fills the door, blocking out the light behind me and cloaking her in shade.

I hunch my shoulders, trying to make myself small. This is only my second visit to Earth, but I know that the people of this planet are uncomfortable with my largeness. I already anticipate the shock of what I have to tell her, and I would soften her alarm by appearing less threatening, less foreign.

"Yes, ma'am. My name is Bati, and I have come to speak with you about your daughter."

It was a smart choice to research proper ways of referring to one's human elders before I came here, and I hope my approach is satisfactory. I hope it eases the fact that I'm a strange man bringing news of her daughter. I brace myself for relief or panic, but instead, the woman rolls her eyes and sucks a breath of air, pulling it loudly through her clenched teeth.

"Lord. Listen, young man. I'm sure you're a good guy, but I do not concern myself with Tiani's affairs. I'm sorry for any misunderstanding you may have about her relationship with you, but if you think I can convince her to keep you, let me just tell you, there's a reason Tee's still single. That girl isn't doing anything she doesn't want to do, and even her mama can't change that."

Her expression is filled with pity. When I scent her, I smell sadness mixed with a tinge of impatience.

"I believe you misunderstand, ma'am—"

"No, I believe *you* misunderstand. You think you're the first young man who's fallen in love with my daughter and come here to convince me that you're the one? Now I don't want to hurt your feelings, but I can assure you that whatever you think is between the two of you means more to you than it does to Tee. The sooner you can realize that, the sooner you can get on with your life and find a young woman who wants to be with you. Tee ain't it."

She's losing patience. I see it in the minute shuffle of her feet, how her eyes keep shifting to the inside of the house, and how the muscles in the arm holding the door flex in preparation to close it. If I am to do as my brother has asked, I must abandon my plan of easing Amina's family into the news of her situation. Otherwise, I may find the door shut in my face before I can explain.

"I bring news of your daughter Amina," I rush out, just as her arm begins to slowly swing the door closed. Her look of patient pity changes immediately to dread. She yanks the door back open and pushes down the handle to the gate, swinging it open with a sudden force that makes me step back before I'm knocked to the side.

"Amina? You've seen her? Is she alright?"

The worry rolling off of this woman is so pungent that I'm filled with a deep sense of shame on behalf of my brother. I have yet to experience the *leht*, but it must be a strong emotion to distract him enough that he waited this long to send further word to Amina's mother. I think of our own mother. How nervous she was while Kwarq was on Earth waiting to reveal himself to his *lehti*. Even then, Kwarq was in constant communication. This woman has not seen or heard from her daughter in weeks. It must be torture for her.

Acting on instinct, I step close and pull her into my arms. My hands cradle the soft, rounded flesh of her shoulders.

"*Ma'h qitah,* Ms. Bennet. My family should have contacted you sooner. I apologize for making you worry."

I know this is against human custom, and unsurprisingly, Amina's mother stiffens in my arms. I hold her gently, keeping my hands light against her body, but initiating enough contact that she can sense my intention. After a moment, she relaxes and my heart aches further when her shoulders twitch with her soft sobs against my chest.

"I just knew something was wrong. That girl has never up and disappeared in her life. That text said she had to go to some other country, but she never told me nothing about that. I just knew something was wrong."

She wraps her arms around my waist and grips me tighter, as if trying to draw the strength to hear what it is I have to tell her. She is a good woman. I can feel it in her energy, and I can smell the warmth and love that radiates around her. It triggers something inside me, and suddenly, I only want to make sure she is never sad again.

"Ms. Bennet, I would explain about your daughter. I assure you, there is less to fear than you believe. Amina is alive and well, but the situation is complicated. Please, if you would permit me inside, I can explain fully."

I ease her away from me. My thin traveling shirt is stained where her face rested. I tilt my head down to peer into her red, puffy eyes. Even distraught, her beauty isn't diminished. If anything, she looks even more delicate than before.

She wipes at her eyes and regards me with sudden suspicion, almost as if this is the first time she has really looked at me. Her head tilts to the side and her expression takes on one that I have noticed on other human women. She has realized that I am strange. That the combination of my features does not quite make sense in this place. She is looking at my blue-black skin, my contrasting light blue eyes. My dark red hair.

"Who are you?"

Her voice is low and careful. I smile as warmly as I can.

"I am the brother of the one who loves your daughter, ma'am. I assure you, Amina has come to no harm. She would have come to relieve you herself, but she has been detained for reasons beyond her control. If you would allow me entry into your home, I can tell you everything you need to know."

Our plan is a risky one. Kwarq warned me before I agreed to come reveal us to Amina's family. We have no way of knowing how her mother and sisters will react. While I don't understand his absence, my task is made easier by the fact that Amina's father does not reside with his family. The men of Earth can be hostile and unyielding. It would be more difficult to peacefully present myself with an aggressive male to contend with.

Fortunately, the women are more open, more inclined to accept the warm feelings of others. Even when I held Amina's mother, she did not rebuff me. Although, I have learned from Amina that this kind of contact is not always welcome among humans.

Amina's mother stares at me for another long moment before she finally steps back into her home, holding the door for me to follow. I duck beneath the threshold and pause at the entrance.

A feeling of intense warmth surrounds me. It seeps through my pores, and I inhale deeply, letting it fill my lungs. Love lives here. It tinges the very air. It's such a contrast to the bitterness of outside that I must be still for a moment and soak it in.

"You have a lovely, warm home," I tell her as I open my eyes. She peers at me like I'm behaving strangely, and I suppose I am. But this is the best feeling I've felt in some time. It's even more enriching than the feeling of my own home, which is always filled with love and laughter and kindness. Something on the air triggers a sense of contentment unlike any I have ever known. It's just a whisper, a suggestion of some happiness I have yet to experience. It lingers on the fringes of the general joy of the dwelling.

"What did you say your name was?"

I shake out of my daze and focus on my mission.

"I am Bati, brother of Kwarq, who is *leht* to your daughter Amina. They have asked me to come here and bring you news so that you do not worry."

"Well, Bati, brother of Kwarq, I need you to sit down because I don't know what you're talking about, and I'm not about to strain my neck looking up at you."

"Ma'am."

I incline my head and follow her into the living room of her home. The space is cluttered in the way that lived in spaces are cluttered. Two long, cushioned seats face each other in front of a fire hearth with a table between them. On the surface of the table are several small replica human vehicles. I lower myself across from Amina's mother, fidgeting as my large body settles into the seat.

"Lord, I hope you don't break my couch. This furniture wasn't made for anyone as big as you." Amina's mother looks worried, but there is an underlying teasing to her tone. I stop moving against the couch and try my best to appear comfortable.

"No, ma'am, your furnishings are completely adequate. I apologize if I have offended you, and I will do my best not to damage anything."

Her comment has made me aware of how small everything on Earth is. I feel like one wrong move could send the entire structure crumbling down around us. Luckily, Lyqa are very precise in our movements. We're large, but graceful. Even in such a small dwelling as this, her belongings are safe from me.

"Now, you tell me where my daughter is because I'm about two seconds away from calling the police."

I can sense her nervousness. She is trying to allay her fears, but her resolve won't last for long. I quickly make the decision to tell her the truth without delay.

"Ms. Bennet, your daughter Amina has joined with my brother Kwarq and currently resides on our home planet, Lyqa."

I relay this information clearly and carefully. I make sure to keep my tone calm and even. Then, I wait for her reaction.

"Who, what, who?"

She's not alarmed. Her scent isn't even fearful anymore. It's impatient.

"I do not want to shock you, but my brother and I traveled to Earth some months ago. While here, Kwarq, my brother, experienced the *leht*, a romantic connection, with your daughter. He persuaded her to accompany him to our planet, Lyqa, and that is where she has been for the past two months. She is well, however. In fact, they have conceived and that is the reason I have been sent in her and my brother's stead."

"Excuse me?"

I smile at her confused expression.

"I am what you would call an alien, ma'am. I am not of this planet, although I would have you know that I mean you no harm. Your daughter is safe with my family and will be here to show you herself in a few days."

"Did you just say you're an alien?"

"Yes, ma'am."

"From another planet?"

"Yes, ma'am."

"And my daughter sent you here to tell me this as an excuse for why she ran off with some man for two months?"

"I do not believe it was her intention run off. Unfortunately, she has entered a resting period due to her conception and is unable to travel until she awakens."

"So, she's asleep?"

"Yes, ma'am, but she is in no risk of harm."

She stares at me with a raised eyebrow. A flush of annoyance spreads beneath the warm brown of her skin.

Amina's mother sucks air through her teeth again and rises. Her movements are angered and jerky. She looks like she is about to run. And while I would never exert any force on another, it would not do well to have this woman run out into the street screaming of aliens and calling for help. I follow her movements toward the door.

"Where is that girl? I bet she thinks this is real funny, but this is not the time for jokes. Just wait until I get my hands on her."

She mumbles these things to herself; although, I can hear her clearly. I relax with the realization that she is not afraid, she just doesn't believe me. I don't think repeating my speech will convince her, so I do the only thing I can. I stand and move to cut her off before she can get to the door. Except, I do not move at human speed. I move Lyqa fast, dashing in front of her before she's had a chance to make it past the living room. She jumps, a high-pitched yelp springing from her mouth. Her hand slaps over her chest, and she stumbles back.

"Ma'am I do not mean to scare you, but I would have you believe me."

Her eyes are wide. I can hear the wild beat of her heart behind her hand. I pay close attention to it. I would not have her alarm cause physical harm.

"Oh, sweet Black Jesus."

She's gasping for air and clutching at her chest. Her fingers catch on a string of beads around her neck, and it snaps. The clatter of the little glass orbs rings loud in the shocked silence.

I step forward and take hold of her arms to steady her. I listen to her heart. It beats fast but there are no irregularities. She's just startled. Her eyes are wide on my face. I take her free hand and press it to my cheek, holding it there so she can feel that I mean her no harm.

"I will not hurt you, but you must believe me when I tell you that I am not of this place. Do you understand?"

Her head jerks up and down. I smell fear on her, but also the slightest bit of excitement. It is the same cautious interest that her daughter had when we first met.

"I will take you to have a seat, ma'am. I know you are afraid, but please do not scream. I would tell you about your daughter. You want to know that she is safe, yes?"

She nods again, and moves stiffly when I lead her back to the couch. I ease her down and sit back across from her. Her eyes never leave me. They stay intent on my face, even as I feel her fear begin to recede just the slightest bit.

"Are you going to abduct me?"

I fight the smile that wants to curve my mouth and shake my head.

"No, ma'am. I will not abduct you. My species is peaceful.

We do not seek to disrupt the happiness of others. I am merely here on the instruction of my brother to give you news that your daughter Amina is safe on Lyqa."

"Where is Lyqa?"

The calmness of her question surprises me. She has managed to compose herself rather quickly.

"It is far, several galaxies away—but do not worry that means you will never see Amina again," I add hastily when her eyes widen again in alarm. "We have very advanced travel technology, and as soon as she has wakened from her resting period, my brother will bring her back here so that you may see for yourself that she is unharmed."

"Awakened? What do you mean? Is she sick?"

"She is not sick, ma'am. She is pregnant. I would be the one to congratulate you on the pending arrival of your grandchildren."

"Amina's pregnant? Oh, my god. How?"

I feel my face warm, and Amina's mother's eyes expand as my skin pulses a bright red. It is a sign of embarrassment for Lyqa, one I have never been good at hiding. I, unfortunately, embarrass easily.

"Ma'am, I would not divulge aspects of my brother's and your daughter's personal interactions, but I believe it occurred in the—natural—way of these things." My skin feels like it's on fire. Embarrassment flares through me like a solar pulse.

"Boy, are you blushing?"

I look up from my flashing hands to find Amina's mother studying at me with disbelief.

"I apologize, ma'am. My people are not uptight about such things, but I did not want to make you uncomfortable."

"Young man, you just walked into my home and told me you're an alien, sped around my living room like something from television, and you're embarrassed to tell me that my daughter's been having sex? Well, ain't that something."

She shakes her head with an expression of wonder. All traces of fear have left her, but there is still a nervous excitement lingering at the edge of her scent. She stares at me for a long moment and then shakes her head again. A small smile lifts one corner of her mouth.

"I got a damn alien sitting in my living room," she chuckles. "I tell you, I can't even be as shocked as I want to be. If anybody was going to find a damn alien to shack up with, it would be one of my daughters. Although, I would have pegged LaShay before Amina. Lord knows Shay is strange enough, but Mina? That girl is usually scared of her shadow."

I smile at the woman's assessment of her daughter. Amina was indeed afraid of many things when she came to Lyqa, but she was also very brave. The way her mother's expression flashes a hint of pride makes it clear she is also aware of her daughter's courage. She continues to look closely at me, her head shaking slightly every few seconds before she puffs out a large breath of air.

"Well, I guess this is real."

"It is," I confirm.

"I still can't believe it, but I can look at you and tell you aren't human."

"I am not," I confirm again.

She leans forward. Her eyes pierce mine.

"And you promise my daughter is okay? You aren't holding her hostage or against her will or something?"

She looks ready to attack me if there is even a possibility that her daughter is not on Lyqa by her own volition. I look over her tiny, round form and can imagine even with my advantage in height, weight, and strength, this woman would do me harm to protect the ones she loves. Lyqa aren't violent creatures, but this need to protect others is an instinct that even we possess.

"I promise. She is well and unharmed. My brother loves her very much and has been caring for her the entire time she has been with us. He will not let harm come to her."

Thinking of my brother's happiness with finding his *lehti* makes me smile. I could not believe at first that the *leht* would bind him to a human, but there is no doubting the happiness my brother feels at having found Amina. As twins, we are more in tune with each other's emotions and feelings, and this has allowed me to share in my brother's new-found joy. The sound of Kwarq's first heart beating strong and steady in his chest has awakened my own curiosity about the *leht*.

"Well, alright then. Alright." She's still trying to convince herself. Every so often her head shakes. "I just can't believe it, but I can't deny what's in front of me, either. So, what's going to happen now?"

A shadow falls across the living room. It's late. I should leave to return to Lyqa. There are other arrangements to make before Kwarq brings Amina back here, and now that my task is complete, I would return to help him.

"I would leave you now, Ms. Bennet. My brother would like to arrange a celebration when we bring Amina back. If it is acceptable, we would bring our parents and older brother to meet you as well."

"You're gonna bring your whole alien family here? To my house?"

I smile again. Humans really do not like the unknown. Although, I imagine Amina's mother is taking this new revelation better than most humans would.

"If you would permit it, I would."

"I mean, do I have a choice? I want to see my daughter."

"Ma'am, if you are uncomfortable with having us here, we will of course see that Amina arrives safely and remain away. I do not deceive you when I say that she is not held hostage.

She may come and go as she pleases. She may choose to never see us again if that is what she wishes."

"And what if she gets here and decides she doesn't want to go back?"

"Then we will leave her here."

"And your brother?"

I smile again. I do not have to guess what Kwarq would do if Amina never wanted to return.

"He would follow her to the ends of the planet if she would have him. Believe me when I tell you that he loves her very much."

"Hm, well, I guess it's okay for you all to come. I probably need to see this all with my own eyes. I still can't believe it."

She sighs and her head shakes again.

"I will go now." I stand slowly and she does too, although her movements are more hesitant and nervous. I round the table and pull her into another embrace. "Thank you for welcoming me into your home and allowing me to speak with you, Ms. Bennet. I look forward to seeing you again."

I give her a gentle squeeze, absorbing again the contentment that floats around her and her home. It's such a peaceful feeling, and as I hold Amina's mother against me, it intensifies, growing quickly so that it is almost overwhelming. I suck in a breath when it morphs into something different. Something stronger and more sensual. It steals over me, suddenly, so that I cannot shake it off. I can only pull Ms. Bennet closer in an effort to get more of it, to pull it into myself, and still, it's like it isn't close enough.

"Young man."

I ease back and blink. The soft, brown face of Amina's mother comes into focus. Her eyes are confused. Embarrassment colors her scent.

"I cannot believe it." My eyes roam over the woman's face, trying to make sense of what I'm feeling. How did I miss it before? How did I not realize the entire time I was speaking to her that this woman is bound to me? I feel it now, getting stronger and stronger every second. The pull, it yanks against my heart straight through the lovely woman in my arms. I know the *leht* knows no bounds, but even I cannot deny that this is an unexpected turn of events.

I smooth my fingers over the faint lines at the corner of Amina's mother's eyes. She scowls. Her mouth moves, but I can only hear the blood rushing through my body and the soft thump of a heart that is not my own.

"Uh, okay. Am I interrupting something?"

My body jerks. The sound of this new voice is like a string, pulling my attention to it. The words are a caress across my senses, and all at once, my breath quickens, just as a surge of pure joy flows through me.

She's standing just behind her mother. I didn't even hear her come in. The pull tightens, and it takes everything in me not to go to her, to lessen the tension, to ease the ache in my chest.

She's staring at me as I stand with her mother locked in my arms. Her dark, nearly black eyes are wide with shock, but a smile plays about her mouth.

Our gazes meet, and I hear the sharp intake of her breath. Her lips move, a movement so slight, so imperceptible that only a Lyqa could see it, and I catch the clearly murmured utterance just as I detect the faint scent of arousal perfume the air: "Damn."

"Young man."

I drag my eyes away from the woman who has captured my heart and look down at her mother, who is still trapped in my rigid embrace. I blink and try to focus on her, even though my mind wants to stay on my *lehti,* a woman so beautiful, I already cannot imagine being without her. It's powerful. My brother did it no justice when he attempted to describe it. This is the best feeling ever.

"Young man?"

"Ma'am?" I answer her respectfully as I focus back on the amused expression of my love.

"That thing poking me better be a flashlight in your pocket, sir."

Chapter 1

TIANI

"You got an eyesight problem?"

Bati's eyes blink slowly over my face. He's staring. He's been staring at me since he got here with his tall, fine family. Even though I've felt his eyes on me every second of the day, I can barely look at him, and not because I don't want to. I do. God, I do. Everything in me is saying climb him like a pole, and that annoys the hell out of me. *He* annoys the hell out of me even as he makes all kinds of dirty things fly through my head.

"I do not know what illness you refer to, but my eye functions operate properly."

I narrow my eyes in annoyance and lean forward before I can stop myself. Of course, he leans forward, too. His mouth curves, and his gaze travels down to check out my cleavage. I mentally shake my head. Men. Even the aliens.

"I thought my sister was teaching you guys Ebonics."

My sister Amina is currently cutting a wedding cake with her alien husband at the edge of our mother's backyard. This would be shocking if it weren't my family. If anyone was going to fall in love with a seven-foot-tall, golden skinned, yellow-eyed alien, it would be my sister. Although, I would have put my money on LaShay before Mina. That just goes to show what the hell I know. I guess I have to admit, though, that so far, these aliens aren't that bad.

"She is teaching my brother," Bati returns and continues to stare me down. Every place his eyes land is like a hot spot on my exposed skin.

They've rigged up some kind of forcefield around the backyard, so even though it's winter outside, the space around our yard is toasty. I'm wearing the only thing I have that's appropriate for a spontaneous, backyard, middle of the night wedding—a strapless red dress with a sweetheart neckline that dips much lower than I wish it would. Especially now that Bati's sitting across from me, looking at me like I'm wearing nothing at all.

"Well, let me give you your first lesson," I shoot back when he continues to stare. "An 'eyesight problem' is what you have when you can't seem to stop staring at someone. You're clearly suffering from one."

He smiles. It's not a cocky smirk. It's a real, full blown smile, and it nearly knocks the air out of me. He's got big teeth. Not really big, but wide. Wider than human teeth, for sure. They shine brightly in the blue-black of his face. His sharp cheekbones tilt up. Heavily lashed eyes sparkle down at me. Damn, this dude is fine.

"If enjoying the face of another gives one a seeing problem, then I will confess to being afflicted with such an ailment," he says with something close to pride.

"I'm serious." My voice is a quiet hiss. He's doing things to me, and I don't like it. I don't like being out of control, and that's all I've been feeling since I met this damn alien. I hate that when I'm in a room with him, I don't know whether to kiss him or kick him. I told Amina he was creeping me out. That was a big fat lie. What his lingering eyes do to me isn't creepy at all, and I'm finding it hard to pretend otherwise.

Amina and Kwarq are still cutting the cake. It's taking longer than it should because Kwarq doesn't really know what to do. He looks confused, but when Amina puts her hand over his and slices through the lower layer, he lets her guide him. His eyes float over my sister's face with so much love that my throat gets a little tight.

He looks at her like this all the time. Like she holds his heart in her hands. Like she's the only person in the world that matters.

"I am also serious," Bati returns, bringing my focus back to him. Not that it ever strayed too far. "I will not deny that looking at you gives me pleasure. You are the most beautiful woman I have ever seen, my *lehti*."

"Yeah, well, didn't anyone ever tell you it's rude to stare?"

"They did not."

I roll my eyes. Of course, they didn't.

"Well, it's rude to stare. I don't like it, so stop looking at me. Got it?"

"Yes, my *lehti*, I will not stare at you if it makes you nervous."

"You *don't* make me nervous."

I don't know why I'm denying it. Of course, he makes me nervous. He makes me more than nervous. He makes me hot. Hotter than I've ever been in my life. I've been giving Bati shit for flirting with me, but I can barely keep myself from jumping across the table and straddling him. I don't know what's wrong with me.

Bati arches a brow, and I lose our little stand off when I look away.

"I can smell you, my *lehti*, and you smell nervous. It is pointless to deny. You cannot hide from me. I will always know what you are really feeling."

My heart ratchets up as his minty breath floats across the

space between us. All these Lyqa folks smell so good. Sweet, like something new. I don't know if this is just some weird alien thing, or if this whole Lyqa household shares the same cologne. Although, something tells me that having super smell would make cologne a bad idea. Maybe that's also why they smell good. All the funky folks probably got bred out.

I take a shaky sip from my glass of champagne. We put this little shindig together in a hurry, but we shelled out on liquor. LaShay and I both agreed that a little buzz might be necessary to deal with an alien wedding. Except, I'm pretty sure LaShay's celebrating. She's at the front, sitting awkwardly close to Kwarq's older brother and sighing dramatically.

"You know it's kind of rude to go around telling people you can smell them," I return finally. "Maybe you should add that as lesson two of things you don't do with humans."

I push back my chair and step away from the table because being this close to Bati makes it hard to remain unaffected by what I'm realizing is some serious Lyqa mojo. I need some distance. A breather is in order if I'm going to survive the night without jumping him.

BATI

Tiani rushes inside, pulling on the door so quickly that it knocks into the side of the house, causing several people to turn. Her mother glances back in displeasure at the retreating back of her daughter. My mother also turns, her eyes gently holding mine. She would have heard the exchange with my *lehti*. My eyes shift to Kwarq.

I have not been paying attention, but for some reason, his face is covered in a layer of the dessert. Amina cackles loudly as she holds a smashed bit of the confection in her hand. I ignore them and stand to follow my *lehti* into the house.

* * *

I hear her the moment I step through the door. Her movements are quick and agitated through the thin walls. I follow the frantic shuffling and heavy handling of objects until I stand inside the doorway of a bedroom on the other side of the house.

The room is hers. It smells of her—a faint, flowery scent that makes my chest flare with warmth. A neatly made bed sits in one corner of the room. It's so small. Perhaps not for a human, but most of my legs would hang off the end of it. My eyes linger on the place where she sleeps, and I imagine what it would be like to lay with her. To feel her wrapped in my arms throughout the night.

She doesn't hear me enter, so I have a moment to watch as she lifts various items from a drawer and packs them into a small cloth bag. She's changed. The beautiful red dress she wore is draped over the foot of her bed. She has exchanged them for a small pair of shorts that show her thick, toned legs and a thin shirt that barely masks the brown skin beneath it. She's still breathing heavily. Her agitation is a fog in the room, but it's underlined with something very close to desire. With hope, I step over the threshold.

"I apologize for making you uncomfortable. It was not my intention, *lehti*."

She pauses with her back to me. Her shoulders heave once, a great heavy sigh that raises the narrow muscles of her back before dropping them back down. When she turns, she's looking at me curiously.

"You know what? I have no idea what's going on, but I really, really want to fuck you, Bati."

It's the first time she has said my name. It triggers a blaze throughout my body, a solar pulse of emotion, that's immediately followed by a powerful thump in my chest. I stand frozen, unable to believe what I'm feeling. Tiani gasps from where she regards me a few feet away. Her hand slaps over the space between her breasts at the exact moment my first heart surges to life.

She clears her throat, massaging her chest with a slight look of panic. Hers would have paused for the briefest moment, one split second of inactivity, before it began to beat again in rhythm with my newly animated organ.

She frowns. I want to tell her that she is okay, but I can only listen to the syncopated music of our hearts. Mine, a deep thud. Hers, a light patter alongside of it. It's beautiful and fills me with such a sense of love and strength that I can barely believe its awesomeness.

"My *lehti.*"

She looks up and shakes her head.

"So, should we just do this? Get it out of the way?"

Her eyes travel from my face, down my body, and then back up again. They flare, briefly, when they get to my middle.

I don't have to look to know what has caused her shock. My first heart is beating, and its primary purpose is to prepare my body to join with my *lehti*. I normally wouldn't display myself so openly to any female, but I can't stop the blood being pumped so furiously to my cock. Even as my brain struggles to return to the conversation, I feel it rising behind my thin travel pants, pulsing with desire. The desire to be where it belongs. Buried deep within my *lehti*. Buried where she is currently inviting me. Even though, her invitation is somewhat...off.

"Lehti?"

She steps closer, peering curiously up at me. I almost step back. Her scent and the desire to pull her to me is so intense that I fear I will not be able to contain myself.

"Do you really not know my name?"

"I do."

"What is it, then?" Her eyes narrow skeptically on me.

"Tiani."

"Good. Then call me by my name. Stop with all that Lettie stuff, okay. Lesson number three. It's rude to call people you don't know random names."

"But you are my *leh*—"

"Buh, buh, buh," she cuts me off, holding the flat of her hand up so that it's right in front of my face. She is closer than she was a moment ago. Her sweet scent fills my nose, flooding my brain, and making it difficult to stand upright. "You don't know me, okay, and it's pretty much going to stay that way. Now, for reasons I can't understand, I'm really, really attracted you. And since you've been staring at me ever since you walked in the door, I'm going to assume that you're really attracted to me, too. So, I'm asking you, as two consenting adults, if you would like to fuck me. Would you?"

Of course, I do. I want nothing more than to lay my *lehti* down and sink into all of her warm places. To savor every part of her, but even in my limited experience with sex, I know this is not what she is offering. She does not want to, as humans call it, "make love." She does not even want the fevered passion of what Kwarq and Amina refer to as "fucking," even though this is what she has called it. What she wants comes without feeling or emotion. It is limited to the moment and offers no potential for things to come. No future. No…love.

It is not what I want with my *lehti*, who I already love so much my bones ache with it. And yet, my cock continues to rise. It continues to prepare for her. Right now, it is thick and straight behind my pants, pointed directly at its target.

Tiani sucks in a breath and lays her small hand over my length and squeezes, trying to make her fingers meet with little success.

"Damn." It's a murmur under her breath that nearly brings

me to my knees it is said with such awe, such reverence. I have researched human male anatomy. I know that, compared to them, Lyqa are—impressive. Still, I never thought that having my first lover, my *lehti,* look upon me with such desire would fill me with pride. Pride that she finds me satisfactory, and eagerness to demonstrate just how much pleasure I can bring her.

"Don't take forever. I'm starting to question whether or not I can even handle this."

She's still holding me. Her hand pumps lightly along the fabric of my pants, and I hiss out a deep breath. Air I didn't even realize I was holding.

"Yes, my *leh*—Tiani. I would very much like to join with you."

She laughs softly and shakes her head.

"We aren't joining." She continues to stroke me. "We're just fucking. I just need to get this out of my system. We don't have to overcomplicate it."

I want to tell her that it is already complicated. That while she may be trying to get her desire for me out of her system, she has already been rooted in my system for my entire existence.

Her hand twists midway up my shaft, setting my skin on edge. I tremble with need. My muscles quiver violently beneath my skin, and both of our gazes widen with shock.

"Is that normal?"

The jerky movement of my head requires all of my effort.

"It is the *leht*. Do not be alarmed. This is just somewhat intense for me."

She smirks and grips me tighter, squeezing until I feel like I'm going to erupt all over my clothes, but then just as quickly, she lets me go and steps back, pulling her top over her head.

"Take off your clothes. We have to hurry so no one comes

looking for us."

I hesitate. Every part of my body wants to follow her instruction, particularly when her small, firm breasts are bared, the dark tips straining up at me, making my tongue swirl in my mouth. I know from my brother that human women find the long, grey tongues of Lyqa strange and perhaps even off-putting, but her smooth, brown flesh only makes me want to taste her. It is a singular thought in my mind, aside from the thought that this moment is wrong. This is not how I want to join with my *lehti*. Rushed and quiet—detached. I do not like it.

"Tiani—" My brain freezes when she slips the shorts down her hips and lets them fall to the floor. My eyes can't take in the taut, toned flesh of her body quick enough. I want to see everything. I want to taste all of her. Specifically, the tantalizing space between her legs that's still shielded from me by a scrape of thinly woven fabric. I inhale deeply and groan.

She is aroused. I can smell her moistness. It's potent and makes it difficult to think clearly.

"Are you just going to stand there, or are you going to get undressed? We don't have all night."

Almost in a trance, I reach for my shirt hem and lift it over my head. My shoulders tense, but I relax when Tiani's eyes flare as the shifting muscles of my chest are exposed.

"Mina wasn't lying when she said you guys were built," she smirks and steps close to me, laying her hands lightly over my hearts. My first heart thumps a steady rhythm beneath my breastbone. My smaller, second heart is a slightly weaker patter beneath it.

"Is that your heart?" she asks, tilting her head to the side as she feels the movement beneath her palms.

"Hearts. I have two."

"Two? That's different. Why do you need two?"

She rubs her hands over the muscles of my chest, flexing her fingers so that the pointed tips of her nails sink lightly into my skin. The sensation is nearly overwhelming, this slight pain mixed with the gentleness of her touch. I hold still and gather myself so that I can answer her questions.

"One heart functions as the primary source of supplying oxygen to the body. My first heart is to serve my *lehti.*"

Her nearly black eyes dance when they look up at me. "What does that mean, serve your lettie?"

"It provides blood to my cock."

Her eyes widen, and she snorts out a short laugh. "Seriously?"

I nod, unable to do much else. Her hands move down to the waistband of my pants, and she toys with the drawstring. She pulls the end of one string, and the fabric at my waist loosens and slides down my hips, only to stop short when it catches the tip of my straining cock.

"You going to do something about that? I kind of feel like I'm doing all the work."

Again, as if working outside of my mind, I reach for the edge of my pants and unhook it, letting them fall to the floor.

"Wow, that is, that's pretty—wow. Good job, first heart."

Tiani reaches to her hips to hook her thumbs beneath the thin straps of her undergarment and pulls them down her legs. She steps out of them, kicking the scrap of fabric to the side, and plants her hands at her hips, staring at me with a bemused expression.

My eyes fall to the space between her round, muscular thighs. Her legs are thick, the outer silhouette curving in an enticing arch from her cinched waist. The inner thighs just meet to cradle her pussy. I want to be there. I inhale again and catch the scent of her sweetness. Help me.

"Are you just going to stand there. Tick tock, remember?" She uses the finger of one hand to tap the bare wrist of the other. I do not know this gesture, but I understand that she is again referring to our limited time together. I don't want to think about that. I don't want to think about the idea that she has already decided that we are not bound for life, or even past this night. My eyes fix to the only thing I want to consider.

"You have not given me permission to touch you," I tell her and hope that she does soon. Although nothing about this joining is as it should be, I can no more turn away from her now than I can turn away from the pull of the *leht*. I want her. If this is the way I can have her, I will accept it. For now.

"Bati, if I didn't want you to touch me, I wouldn't have said let's fuck."

I shake my head. There are some things I will not compromise on.

"I want to hear you say it."

"You can touch me," she returns with a confused smile. Her hands go to her hips again and her plump little breasts shake. I swallow and force myself to keep her gaze.

"Thank you, Tiani. Now I want you to say that you want me."

"What?" Her head jerks back. Her eyes shift back into her head, and she huffs out a deep breath. "Look, do you want to do this or not?"

"I do, but I will not do it if you cannot admit that you truly desire me. I would know that you desire me as much as I desire you."

She stares at me for a long moment, and I worry that she will snatch her clothes from the floor and exit the room. As much as I do not want that to happen, I will not join with her if she is acting out of mere curiosity.

"Fine, I want you." It's reluctant, but the faint flush of blood that my Lyqa sight detects beneath her brown skin leaves no mistake that she is telling the truth. Almost immediately after the admission leaves her, the sweet, tangy perfume of her arousal increases ten-fold. It hits me like a fist to the chest, staggering my control, so that it takes all of me not to toss her to the bed. Instead, I step closer and lean down to press my mouth to hers.

Amina is small. My brother towers over his *lehti,* dwarfing her with his height and the bulk of his size. Tiani, by comparison, is taller and slightly thinner than her sister, but she is still human. Compared to my Lyqa form, she is delicate enough to break. As our lips melt gently together, I take hold of her arms, and I'm shocked at how slight she feels in my hands.

"Open for me," I whisper against the soft pillows of her lips. She leans up and nips at my bottom lip, pulling it between her tiny, white teeth. Again, this edge of discomfort only serves to arouse me more, and I press in, sweeping my tongue into her mouth.

"Mm," she moans around my tongue. Remembering my brother's advice, I give her just enough, stroking along the soft tissue of her mouth, tangling with her shorter, blunter tongue. With each stroke, I sense her arousal heightening.

"You're a good kisser for an alien," she murmurs when we ease apart. Her eyes droop with passion. The black, bottomless irises stare up at me.

"You do not find my tongue to be strange?"

She shrugs. "A little, but it's not a deal breaker."

I am glad this is not a 'deal-breaker' because there are other places I would put my slightly strange tongue.

"Can I taste you, Tiani? I cannot wait much longer, and I need to prepare you more for our joining."

She smiles up at me. Her mouth curving sweetly. "Are you asking to eat me out?"

I do not know this expression, but I don't have to wonder what it means. It matches perfectly with how I'm feeling. I want to consume her. I want to taste and nibble and lick every part of her. If this isn't a kind of hunger, I do not know what is.

"I want to lick your pussy, yes."

Another wave of arousal rises from between our bodies. She likes this, my *lehti*. She is stimulated when I speak explicitly to her.

Her breathing catches as she looks up at me, but she doesn't move. I step forward, prompting mirrored steps from her, until she reaches the bed and collapses back. I fall over her, catching my weight with my forearms.

I cover her mouth again, sweeping deeply with my tongue. Giving her more of me until she pushes at my chest, gasping and laughing slightly.

"Dude, I have to breathe."

I kiss her mouth gently as she sucks in deep lungfuls of air. Each inhale brushes her nipples against my chest, and I can wait no longer to taste her all over.

I kiss down the side of her smooth neck, pleased when a breathy sigh sounds out above me. I linger, lapping at the silky flesh, sucking softly then harder, until the heat rises beneath her skin. When I lift away, there's a deep, purple mark where the blood has been pulled to the surface. A sense of intense possession fills me, even as I know she is not yet mine, that she has not yet given herself to me truly.

I move down until the tight peaks of her breasts dip and swell beneath my mouth. She's breathing quickly, and yet I still feel restraint in her. As if she seeks to get away from me, to get away from what she would feel. She grips the sheets until her knuckles appear ready to pierce her skin.

I pause, letting my breath whisper over her fevered skin. Her legs twitch beneath mine, perfuming the air with her sweet scent. I close my eyes, groaning at the lust that flares within my body. My mouth waters at the thought of having her on my tongue. Of knowing every intricacy of her taste across my hundreds of thousands of taste buds.

"Bati!"

This desperate cry is what I'm waiting for. It spurs me into action, and I flick my tongue out, swirling it around the dark, tight nipple before closing my mouth over the sweet tip and drawing hard.

"Ah!" Her cry is high and tortured. She gasps and leans away, but then shifts closer again, arching her back up and pressing herself into my mouth.

I don't relent. I kiss and lap at every bit of skin I can, drawing hard on her nipple until she curves her fingers into my tight cap of curls and yanks my head over to her other breast. I chuckle softly. She may wish to distance herself from how much she desires me, but nothing will happen between us unless she initiates it.

I move to her other breast under the guidance of her hands and slowly drag my tongue around the plump mound before drawing firmly on the tip. I continue in this way, moving back and forth between her breasts, savoring the fragrant valley between them, nipping and licking, until she starts to squirm beneath me again. She shifts up, causing her nipple to pull wetly from my mouth.

"More. Move down."

"Move down to where, Tiani."

I rest my chin on her soft belly. Her eyes narrow on me in restrained lust.

"You know where."

"I do not."

She holds my gaze, and the emotional war on her face is so obvious that I can only just keep from shaking my head. I don't know why my *lehti* is so determined to keep herself from me. As I expect, her face firms and determination scents her skin. I flick my tongue out to taste it, and she gasps when her muscles twitch.

"I didn't think I'd have to spell it out, but since it looks like I have to, I want you to lick my pussy? There. You happy?"

"I am."

I really am. Being this close to the space between her legs is almost too much. Still, I take my time, easing down the bed until my face hovers over the moist, trim patch of hair that covers the place where I want to be forever. I want to wait. To torture her a little bit more, but her scent hits me full force and it's too much.

I extend my tongue, letting each inch curl from my mouth, and I drag it slowly up the middle of her slit.

"Oh fuck!" Tiani lurches off the bed, and when I look up, she's staring at me between her legs, her face a mask of confusion. Our hearts beat quickly. I keep my eyes on hers as I lap through her folds, curling my tongue to catch the hardened little nub at the top.

"Ah!" Tiani's head falls back before it jerks back up again. She frowns. Almost in annoyance. "What are you doing to me?"

I feel her genuine bewilderment.

"I am tasting you." I demonstrate by nudging the tip of my tongue at her entrance. She moans and watches me behind lowered lids. Her legs twitch around my head.

"Fuck, hold on. I can't—" She doesn't finish because I close my lips over the taut little bud peeking from her folds and suck, swirling my tongue against her as she gasps and cries out, her body jerking. "Bati, wait, ohmygod!" She lurches off the bed. Her legs tremble violently as her release pulses through her. I see her through it, lapping at her quivering flesh, savoring the pleasure rolling off of her. Savoring her taste as it gushes onto my tongue.

I raise my head when she finally relaxes. The air of the room hits my face, cooling the moisture around my mouth.

Unthinking, I swipe my tongue out, trying to catch every bit of her that I can.

"Holy shit." Tiani's eyes are wide. I grow warm and pull my tongue back.

"I apologize. I know my tongue is somewhat stran—"

In one smooth motion, Tiani flips around to her knees and presents her round, plump bottom to me. I gulp down the words as she lowers her chest to the bed, pushing out the slick, swollen folds of her pussy.

"Fuck me, Bati," she demands, arching back. I can't tear my eyes away from the juicy slit before me. The thick flesh of her thighs presses it together, giving just a glimpse of that enticing bud. My already straining cock grows even harder until my pelvis aches with the pull of it. "Please, I need—hurry!"

Tiani's urgent cry snaps me from my trance. I crawl forward on my knees until the crown of my cock is kissing the lips of her opening.

I smooth a hand over her behind, and I'm pleased that even my large palm cannot cover its entirety. I knead the plump flesh and the urge to stroke my cock and mark her beautiful, brown skin with my seed makes the tip weep a little droplet of sperm against her pussy.

"I will try to be gentle, Tiani, but I am large, and it will be uncomfortable for you initially." I use every bit of my effort to will control over my body. What I want to do is press every inch of my cock through her dripping folds until I am so far inside of her that we become one.

"Bati, I can take it. Just do it!"

Without warning, Tiani presses back. Her pussy lips part around the thick head of my cock and her warmth constricts me as I squeeze through the first several inches of her passage.

"Fuck!" Tiani's word is a sharp shout. I only vaguely think

that most of the people outside, definitely my family, will have heard it. She pauses, her pussy clasping around me and sending shock waves of pleasure through my body. It is almost too much to bear and more than I imagined for my first joining. I smooth a hand down her back. Her body is tense, and I feel her discomfort.

"*Lehti*, are you okay?"

Her breaths are deep inhales and loud expulsions of air against the pillow beneath her head.

"Sssss, my name isn't Lettie," She hisses softly and rocks her hips back, seating me another inch. A groan rumbles in my chest. Even being inside of her these few inches is magic.

"Ah, Tiani, you feel better than I ever could have imagined. So tight and perfect." I clench my teeth as she rocks back to take me further. My hips move of their own accord to meet her, and she gasps when I slide in several more inches.

"Bati, do it. Go all the way."

I look down to where our bodies are joined. She's stretched taut around me, and already I can feel her flesh tightening further. My cock shines with her juices when I pull from her sweet body, and suddenly, I only want to be deep inside of this warm, wonderful place. I take hold of her hips, keeping them steady in a firm grip and surge forward, pushing my way through the tight warmth of her pussy until I'm pressing against her womb.

"Mmn!"

"Arrrrrhg!" The groan that meets her moan is guttural and stuttered. My entire body shakes from the intensity of being joined with my *lehti*. I still, giving her a moment to adjust.

"More," she gasps out, pushing even further back onto my cock. I send a plea to the universe to help me maintain control. I would give her everything.

Rocking my hips back, I press open the soft cheeks of her bottom to watch as my shaft reappears from her body. My

Lyqa senses catch every sensation. The slick, textured flesh of her passage, the feathery scrape of the short hair covering her lips. It sends a billion bolts of pleasure through me. I sink back in before pulling out to do it again.

"You are made for me, Tiani," I declare as I drive in and out of her, my eyes fixed to the action of our joining. She moans every time I reach her end. "Did you hear me? Your pussy was made for my cock."

I don't know why I need to tell her this, but I do. Despite offering herself to me, she has made it a point to shield her feelings, to insist on detachment. But we are joined now, I think, as I continue to thrust my cock into her. We are attached in the most meaningful way aside from the *leht*.

"Bati, stop talking," she gasps out as I slide into her again. She tries to insert admonishment into her tone, but she smells of excitement and something else I cannot decipher. This lie, asking me to be silent when she really enjoys what I'm saying, makes something defiant rise in me, and I lean over her, until my mouth is over her ear, never slowing my hips.

"You cannot lie to me, my *lehti*. Do you hear that? Do you hear how wet you are for me? Your pussy knows it was made for my cock even if you deny it."

"Ah, you jerk!" she screams, just as her body clenches around me and she shakes with another orgasm. It's too much for me. My hips speed up, and my cock starts to spurt before I even realize what's happening.

"Lehti!"

Stream after stream of semen shoots into her. The muscles in my back tense as my balls draw up firmly. My body spasms for several long moments, until finally, the last spurt signals the end to my release. I collapse back, sliding from Tiani's body and coming to rest against the wall.

I can barely move. Tiani is still bent over, and again I am drawn to the puffy slip of her pussy. I feel a moment of disappointment when my seed drips in a steady stream from her body. I scented the hormones to prevent conception on Tiani before we joined. I do not insert myself in a female's right to dictate the uses of her womb, but I can't help the longing that rises in me to have my seed take root. To start a family.

A scent hits my nose. It's fear. Tiani hasn't moved, and I shift to my knees and stretch around to view her face. Why is she frightened?

"Tiani, are you all right? Did I hurt you?" This first joining was intense. Before my release, I lost myself for a moment, thrusting into her wildly. She seemed to enjoy it, but if I hurt her, I will never forgive myself.

Her eyes focus on me, and when they do, I'm shocked by the terror I see in them.

"Dude, what the fuck did you just put into my body?"

TIANI

"My cock?"

I mentally amend my opinion of Bati's ignorance being kind of cute. It's not. My ass is still in the air, and my pussy is still leaking whatever weird, alien fluid he just four-minute long jizzed into me, but I'm too scared to move. Whatever he's left in there is squishing around. It's like I have a mini ocean in my cooch.

"Bati, what the fuck did you just come in me?"

His frown is a strange kind of smile because I'm still on my head.

"I do not know what you mean, Tiani. I merely released. I apologize for not consulting you first, but it happened—suddenly. I did not have time to prepare my exit."

His eyes shift away from me for a moment, and his skin

does something that makes my eyes widen further. He starts to pulse a soft pink color. It fades in and out, and I'm reminded of a mood ring when you dip it in cold water.

"Why are you turning pin—oh my god, what is that!"

More of the thick liquid gushes from my body and I freeze, digging my nails into the sheet. I can't believe I let this alien cum in me. He probably just laid an egg in me or something. I try to think back to what Amina has told me about Lyqa, which isn't much, except they have huge dicks and are great lovers. She got pregnant the first time they fucked. Instantaneously, she said. I'm on the pill, but who knows if that even matters.

"Tiani, what you are feeling is my seed. Because you are preventing your body from conceiving, it has no place to go and must come out. It may be more comfortable if you come off of your head."

Right, I'm still bent over with my ass in the air like an idiot. I lift up, moving carefully, and ease onto my butt. The continued flow of sperm from my pussy makes me scrunch my face up in thinly veiled disgust.

"Do human males not ejaculate?" Bati sits near me on the bed, his expression a mixture of concern and confusion.

"They do, but not this much. You came for like three minutes. I feel like there's a gallon of sperm in me."

"Lyqa males do not usually release so much. It is only due to the *leht*, and my body's preparation to produce young, that my semen is so plentiful."

He's doing that weird pulsing thing again. I have no idea what he's talking about. He's been bringing up this *leht* thing since I met him, but I haven't really asked about it. And I'm not going to. I find the easiest way to avoid complication in my interactions with men is to keep the sharing to a minimum. Essential information only. I'm sorry, did he just say, "produce young"?

"Wait, you better not be trying to get me pregnant. I'm on the pill. It will still work with you, right?"

"It will," he confirms, his face shifting into a little scowl. "I would never interfere with your prevention of conception, Tiani. That is not my choice to make. Any efforts to conceive will be decided upon together."

He had me until that last part. Still, it's such an atypical thing for me to hear from a man, that I can't help but feel relief.

"Thank you for that. Honestly, I never have unprotected sex, but, um, Amina said that you all don't have sexually transmitted diseases, so."

"We do not."

"I'm also clean. I mean, I've been tested. I don't have anything. I guess we probably should have discussed it. I kind of got away with myself." I'm stuttering and it annoys me. Sex is easy. I'm never nervous talking about sex. I also don't mind the awkward safety conversations that go along with it. Still, I feel myself get a little flustered. I would never admit it to him, but I was glad when I remembered Amina said they didn't carry STIs. For some reason I can't explain, I wanted there to be nothing between me and Bati.

Another gush of liquid brings my mind back to the business happening between my legs, and I pull my knees up to my chest, wincing when the effort produces a sharp ache throughout my lower body. This dude kind of went to town on my pussy.

"That was probably the best sex I've had in my life, so I hate to tell you this, but this whole ten gallons of cum thing is gross, buddy." My grimace intensifies as the puddle beneath me grows larger. I can't bring myself to move. I shift my eyes back up, and they come to rest on a smiling Bati.

"I am your best lover?" His smile widens, and I swear his chest puffs up. I guess men are the same no matter what planet they're from. Still, there's no use in lying. He must know he's a good lay.

"You are. I don't mind admitting it. Although, I was led to believe that Lyqa weren't the gloating type," I return dryly.

Bati's smile shifts quickly down, and suddenly he looks shy.

"Before tonight, I had not joined with anyone. I am merely happy that I have pleased you. I would have it that I always please you."

Lyqa are pretty flowery with their use of English. It takes me a minute to sort through everything he's said, and when I do, my internal groan is loud.

"Oh, my god," I cover my face with my hands. Please don't let me have heard that right. "Did you just say that you were a virgin?"

"I do not know what that is."

I peek through my fingers. He's staring at me in confusion. My eyes roam over the broad expanse of his chest where his muscles flex and bunch beneath the smooth dark skin. His dick is soft, but it still hangs heavily in his lap. Just thinking about how hard he pounding into me, how perfectly he stroked along my walls sends a shiver through me. There's no way it was his first time.

"It means you've never had sex before. I thought you were saying that this was your first time having sex."

"It was," he replies frankly. The expression on his face remains calm and open.

"I'm the first person you've had sex with? This is the first time your dick has ever been in a pussy?"

His expression doesn't change. "You are, and it is. And if I may say, your pussy was worth the wait. I have never felt something so incredible as being inside of you."

His words make my skin all jittery, and even though my pussy is still oozing alien jizz, I begin to soften. He's distracting me. I snap my brain back to attention.

"Why the hell haven't you had sex before?" It comes out as an accusation. Mostly because I'm hot again, and I don't want to be. This was supposed to be a one and done, a way to get him out of my system. To get over this pull I've been feeling to him since I caught him with my mother in our living room a couple of weeks ago. I should be over him like I would be over any other man, but I'm not. If anything, I want to lay back and let him fill me up again. As I focus on getting my emotions under control, Bati's mouth quirks up at one corner.

"I was waiting for my *lehti*. I wanted to only share the beauty of a joining with her. Shall we join a second time?"

"What?"

"I can smell you. You are aroused again."

"I am not." It's a weak denial. I'm panting. I don't know why I want it so bad, but I do. Bati tilts his head to the side and looks questioningly at me.

"Why do you lie?"

"Excuse me?" My head rolls back on my neck of its own accord. Who the hell does he think he is to point out the obvious?

"You lie," he repeats like I didn't just hit him with my most threatening glare. "You hold yourself away from me. You say you only want sex, but our heart beats with longing when I am near. You ignore your desire even as your pussy grows wet and hungry for my cock. Why do you do this?"

"Why do you say things like that?" I hate the way my voice falters. I hate it almost as much as I hate that he's a little right.

"Do you prefer I not speak truthfully to you? Would you rather I pretend not to want you? Do as you attempt and hide my feelings?"

"I'm not hiding anything. I don't even know you. The only feeling I had toward you was lust, buddy, and after this shit,"

I point to my dripping cooch, "I'm not in a rush for a repeat." I am in a rush, though. He's right. I'm a liar, but not about liking him. I don't like him. I like his dick, and the expert way he licks my pussy with his creepy ass tongue, but I don't like him. Not really.

I raise a triumphant eyebrow, but Bati merely continues to stare me down. I wonder for a moment if I've hurt him with my comment about his jizz, but then his mouth turns up into that knowing smile, and I want to pop him.

"I told you, Tiani. You cannot hide from me. I will always know the truth of what you feel."

Chapter 2

BATI

"It sounded like at least one of us had an exciting night," Ah'dan comments as I walk into the room Tiani's mother has given us to share during our stay. It is small and with two adult Lyqa males, cramped. We can barely move without bumping into one another, so unfortunately, I cannot escape Ah'dan's interrogation. Nor can I cuff him as I wish to without triggering a brotherly brawl that would most certainly result in the destruction of all of our new mother-in-law's furnishings.

"My night was very exciting," Kwarq cuts in. We share a glance, and I smile at his attempt to deflect attention from me. "You should consider performing the human proposal tradition with Tiani. The women were particularly moved by it. I also believe that Amina feels properly bound to me since we got married."

"I do not think Tiani is quite prepared to commit herself to me in such a way," I admit reluctantly. It is clear I will not have as easy a time as Kwarq had with Amina in getting Tiani to accept the *leht*. As yet, I have not even explained our attachment, and she does not seem keen to know. Her insistence on keeping things between us "casual" is somewhat frustrating. I want her to know of my love. I want to bend my knee for her as Kwarq did for his *lehti*.

"Well, she was eager enough to commit herself in other ways," Ah'dan inserts in the way that he must. I cut my eyes to him, but do not respond, to which he smirks and arches a brow. "Come now, brother. Will you force me to continue making comments, or will you share? Kwarq shared when he met his *lehti,* and you were too eager to hear what he had to say."

"I understand now his reluctance to give us details of his interactions with Amina. It is incredibly private."

Ah'dan rolls his eyes and pulls a face. "You two are not as fun as you were before. I never behaved this way. I was very forthcoming," he pouts, looking almost like a child.

It's true, but it's also true that since I realized Tiani was my *lehti,* I have felt less concerned with trivial things as before. My only concern now is loving and protecting her.

I can feel Tiani in the kitchen. I can smell the meal she is preparing. I can sense the satisfaction she feels with completing the task of feeding her family.

I still can't believe the awesomeness of the *leht*. Our hearts keep a steady rhythm. I listen to her breathing. The tinkling sound of her laughter as she speaks with her sisters. I have been keeping an ear on her all day, unable to stop myself from checking every moment to be sure she is well and happy.

However, Ah'dan is right. The distraction of feeling for my *lehti* has meant I am not behaving as my usual playful self. I'm worried about Tiani's reception of me. Both of my brothers have been *leht*. Perhaps it would be good to receive some advice on winning Tiani over.

"I do not know that Tiani wishes to have a relationship with me," I admit. "She was very eager to join, but not so eager to address the attraction between us. Was it this way with Amina?"

Kwarq's brows furrow. "Amina was afraid of my not being human initially and worried about our family's acceptance of her, but she did not reject the *leht*. She was less believing of the fact that I love her as much as I do. Perhaps it is the same with Tiani. Maybe you need to reassure her of your feelings."

"Perhaps," I respond. Although, I don't think this is the solution to my problem.

"Or maybe you need to reassure her that there is no rush for her to accept you. That worked with Amina."

This is a good idea. Tiani has a warmth to her, I can feel it. I can smell it. But she does not seem as ready to share her love as Amina. It appears, I will have to work for her acceptance.

TIANI

"So, what was with all that ruckus last night? You couldn't wait until after my wedding to get dick-downed by my brother-in-law?"

"What?"

My sister Amina squeezes past where I'm standing making breakfast. Her tight, round belly pushes into my back, and I press closer to the stove, making sure my shirt doesn't catch on fire.

Amina's been lingering around me for the past ten minutes. I've had to restart breakfast twice because every time I put a cooked piece of food down, she eats it. Apparently, a side effect of being pregnant by an alien is that she wants to eat everything in sight. I slide my spatula under one of the pancakes on the griddle and flip it onto the empty serving plate where not two minutes before there were five pancakes. Amina swoops in and snatches the fresh one up, folding the entire thing into her mouth. I sigh.

"Look, I'm not about to do this all day. How much more are you going to eat?"

I'm not really annoyed with her, but it doesn't matter because her face turns down and she opens her mouth, letting the half-eaten pancake fall back onto the serving plate with a wet splat.

"Ugh, nothing. I'm over it."

My stomach flinches, and I swallow down the bile that rises in my throat. "I'm sorry, were we raised by wolves? You marry an alien and suddenly you don't have any home training?"

We both stare down at the slimy ball of dough. Amina grimaces and turns away before lifting the plate and flipping it over the trash. The pancake hits the plastic with a dense thud, and her body lurches involuntarily like she's going to be sick.

"Sorry, Tee. Believe me, if I could help it, I would. This shit is weird as hell, but I really can't control it. It's literally like something takes over me. I don't mean to be gross."

She rinses the plate at the sink and sets it back down. We both stare at it for a second before she opens the cabinet to pull down a fresh plate before placing the other one into the dishwasher. Almost at the same moment, we burst out laughing.

"I didn't want to say anything," I confess around a chuckle.

Amina tosses her head back, a loud cackle erupting from her throat. "Look, I can't even look at that plate."

I slide the rest of the cooked pancakes onto the new plate and pour another batch. My eyes fix to the little bubbles that blister the surface of the batter.

"I'm still waiting for my answer."

This girl can't let anything go. I flip the pancakes first and when I answer, I keep my voice neutral.

"To what?" Right about now, I wish a side effect of being knocked by an alien was minding your own business.

"Tee, you know my man is Lyqa, right? Lyqa as in super spidey-hearing, super-fast. As in, if I sneeze a block from here and it sounds too aggressive, he will literally be there in two seconds flat to make sure I'm okay. His whole family was like a bunch of glow worms last night after you two disappeared inside. His parents flashed so bright Mom thought they were about to explode or something."

"Is that what that is, when they turn red, embarrassment?"

"Yup. Now stop changing the subject cause the way Kwarq kept looking at your bedroom window, there's no way you guys weren't doing something."

I drop the spatula to the counter and turn to face her. She's waiting with raised eyebrows. Her hand moves in a slow circle over her stomach. I think about when I was pregnant. How tight I felt. How heavy. My mind focuses on something I've been trying to ignore all morning, the little puddle of dampness in my panties courtesy of what's left of Bati's cum. I shift my legs uncomfortably. I probably should have changed my clothes, but I don't want to. I like feeling him there. I like remembering what he felt like inside of me.

"Yeah, so, we fucked. What do you want me to say?"

She looks guiltily away before meeting my eyes again. "Honestly?"

"Can I stop you?"

She rolls her eyes, but continues anyway. "I want you to say you aren't going to break his heart."

My head jerks back. And as if responding to her words, my heart stutters for a second. I press my hand to the flat of my chest, and Amina's eyes shift to the spot briefly.

"What are you talking about?"

Her eyes slide away again. Her lips pull in like they do when she's trying not to tell something.

"I'm just saying, be careful with him."

"I'm always careful." I can't stop the bite that creeps into my response.

"Well, you're always careful not to let things go further than you want, but Lyqa aren't like humans. Some things are a bit more literal for them."

My eyes rotate to the side and back again. "Okay. I never told the man that we were gonna get married. It was just sex. I'm pretty sure he understood that." I'm not sure. When I think about the things he said while he was inside of me, I wonder if I'm the one being naive.

Amina fidgets a bit more. I can tell she isn't saying something, and even though it might be something I should know, I wonder if I even want to.

"Just be careful with him, okay? I love Kwarq, and I love his family. I know how you are about relationships, and I'm not trying to convince you to give it a chance—even though you won't regret it—but if you're not going to take him seriously, be upfront about it and be, you know, nice."

"I'm always nice." I may be clear about my intentions with people, but I'm not cruel. I don't string people along, and I don't lie about what I want. Usually. I may have told a small lie, recently.

Amina's head shifts to the side, and a look of pity flashes across her face. "Oh, no, sweetheart. You aren't nice at all. You're kind of a cold-hearted, heart breaker, Tee."

"Are you serious?"

"What are we talking about, how Tee be ruining these dudes' entire existences and leaving them withering in the dirt behind her?"

Our youngest sister LaShay trudges into the kitchen. Her arms extend over her head on a stretch. She yawns deeply and plods past us to the fridge, ignoring my indignant stare, and pulls out the carton of orange juice.

"What do you mean? I don't ruin anybody."

LaShay snorts as she lifts her cup to her lips, draining the glass in one big gulp. She works up a loud belch and sets the cup back on the counter to pour a second glass.

"Girl, please, you stay breaking dudes' hearts."

My eyes shift back to Amina, but she just twists her mouth up to the side and looks away. LaShay picks up a pancake and takes a bite, shrugging her shoulders.

I snort and fold my arms over my chest. My heart's beating very fast. It's also really loud. I hate the idea that there could be some truth to what they're saying.

"Name one guy whose heart I've broken," I challenge, raising a brow at them.

"Torrian," LaShay shoots without hesitation.

"Andre," Amina follows right behind her.

"Andre number two."

"Good one." Amina gives it up to Shay with a point.

"Keith."

"DeAngelo."

"Medium Mike."

"That was second grade," I counter, but Shay shrugs her shoulders again.

"Doesn't matter. You still broke his heart."

"All I did was tell him I didn't want to go with him."

"In the middle of the lunch room," LaShay returns.

"And then you called him dusty," adds Amina with a smirk.

"He asked me why I didn't want to go with him," I contend.

"Yeah, but you're supposed to say cause you don't want to or you already go with somebody. You're not supposed to say it's cause he's dusty."

"But he was."

"Tee, you made him cry," LaShay reminds me.

"In front of the whole school," continues Amina.

"He transferred," LaShay finishes.

"Oh, my god! Now that was not my fault," I huff out.

"Face it, when it comes to men, you're kind of mean," LaShay states matter-of-factly and pats my shoulder. I jerk out from under her hand.

"Well, you know what? You can't tell me that all of those men, even Medium Mike's dusty ass, didn't deserve it if I was. Not one of them was worth shit."

I'm satisfied when LaShay shrugs and nods her head in agreement. Even Amina looks like she's about to relent, but then she stares pleadingly at me.

"Yeah, but Bati isn't like that. He really is a good guy, and he probably cares about you a lot already. Did he explain about the *leht*?"

"Nope, and I didn't ask him, and I'm not going to. I asked if he wanted to fuck, he said yes. I made sure he knew that's all it was, and he agreed. Whatever he feels after that is his own problem. What's the big deal about this whole let thing anyway?"

Amina huffs out a breath and covers her face in frustration. I can tell she wants to tell me, but something is stopping her. She opens her mouth to speak before LaShay cuts her off.

"What! You fucked Kwarq's brother? How did I miss that? Is he packing? Was it good? Is he as fine all over as he is in the face?" Shay's barrage of questions don't leave room for me to answer. Her eyes widen as she continues in a low whisper. "Are you pregnant, now, too?"

"What, no! I'm on birth control," I return, but my thighs twitch around the wetness in my panties.

"How do we know birth control is enough to stop Mount Olympus Lyqa sperm?"

"Trust me, if she was pregnant, she would know." Amina rubs over her stomach for emphasis. Two months ago, it was flat as a board. Now she's due to give birth to twins in a matter of days. "Anyway, about the *leht*. It's better if he explains it," she continues, but then reaches out to cover my hand with one of hers. The look on her face is urgent. "Just, please, promise me that you will either leave him alone or give him a chance for real. But if you really want nothing to do with him, please, please, be nice about it, and don't keep fucking him. *Please*!"

Amina is definitely the most sensitive of us sisters, but even she doesn't sweat cutting a dude off. That she's so concerned I might hurt Bati makes me give in.

"Fine, I promise, but it doesn't matter because now that you're acting so weird about it, I'm definitely not going to fuck him again."

Chapter 3

TIANI

"Tiani, did you sleep well?"

I jump at the sound of Bati's voice behind me. I'm in the walk-in pantry off our kitchen looking for any vegetables I can use to make breakfast for the Lyqa. Amina conveniently forgot to mention that they don't eat meat until after I made an entire pack of turkey bacon. It didn't matter. She got caught in another hungry spell and nearly ate the whole pack before I had time to save some for the rest of us.

The pantry isn't small, but with a Lyqa in it, it feels about the size of a cardboard box.

Bati's broad shoulders block out the view of the kitchen behind him. He and his brothers are so gentle that it isn't until you really look at them that you realize how big they are. My eyes travel up from the bit of bluish-black muscle peeking through the deep V in Bati's shirt to his face. The top of his head is almost to the ceiling.

"I slept fine. Why are you sneaking up on me?" My voice is harsher than I want it to be.

"I am not. I could hear your sounds of exasperation. I thought perhaps I could help with whatever is troubling you." His reply is easy. His expression never changes.

I was huffing and puffing in here. My mother likes to keep the emergency canned foods on the top shelf, and even at my unusually tall for my family height of five-seven, I can't reach them.

"Oh, yeah. I'm trying to find something for you guys to eat since you're vegetarians. I didn't know. I made bacon."

He cocks his head to the side. "Bacon?"

"It's the food of the gods and delicious, but it's made from animal so you guys can't eat it," I inform him. His mouth shifts up a little as I speak, and I have to tear my gaze away from his full lips. He really is damn fine. I clear my throat. "Anyway, if you grab me those four cans in the front up there, I can make you all a succotash." I point up to the top shelf and avoid his lingering gaze.

He continues to stare at me as he reaches up, barely stretching his arm, to grab the cans of corn, okra, and stewed tomatoes I've pointed out. As he does so, he takes the tiniest step forward, and I close my eyes to gain control over my traitorous body. I'm on fire, and not just because he's so close that his body heat radiates directly into me. The desire to throw myself against his body is nearly irresistible. My nipples harden. I'm still in my pajamas, and the worn, threadbare t-shirt is doing nothing to hide the tight peaks behind my shirt. In some kind of weird chain reaction, my pussy clenches, and a fresh gush of wetness leaks between my legs.

Bati's holding the cans in front of me. I reach out to take them but he pulls them back out of my grasp. My eyes jump to his, and the bright blue flares. His eyes are blue? I didn't notice before, but I do now. They're bright little gems in the smooth darkness of his face. He takes a deep breath.

"Mm." It's a low rumble in his chest. My own breath hitches when I realize what's just happened. He's smelled me. I try to tell myself that's gross, but it's not. It's hot, and it only makes my pussy more slippery.

His lips move. A few wispy sounds just reach my ears.

"What was that? A prayer?" I don't know what I'll do if this man was just praying to his Lyqa god for strength. Even I'm not immune to that kind of flattery.

His eyes burn into mine so that I couldn't look away if I wanted to. He takes another step closer, and my rapidly rising chest meets his with each breath. His head shakes slowly from side to side.

"I was telling my brother not to allow anyone to enter your kitchen."

Oh shit. I know what's coming. I feel it with every thud of my heart, and I want it. Even as I feign ignorance.

"Why'd you do that?"

One of his hands slides around my waist to hoist me up against his chest. I brace myself with my hands against his pecs, and I'm forced to offer up my own little prayer to the universe for sending me a man this fine. No, I remind myself. He isn't my man. He's just *a* man, with a penis I like. Very much.

"Because I can smell that you want me, and I would not deny you anything that you want."

I don't know what comes over me, but I lunge at him, attacking his mouth with mine. I moan around the smooth, thin length of his tongue when he pushes past my lips, swiping along the inside of my mouth in tickling brushes. He turns his head, cradling the back of my neck with his other hand as he deepens the kiss. His tongue rolls out to the back of my mouth, and I'm not even grossed out.

I need more. I yank at the top of his shirt, trying to get my hands through the V. I want his warm skin beneath my palms. He pulls away from our kiss with a chuckle and stills them.

"Although, I imagine that at least my family will hear us, it would not do for me to leave the kitchen looking as if I have been attacked." He kisses my knuckles before releasing my hands and lifting the hem of his shirt over his head in one smooth motion. My mouth hangs open as inch after inch of shimmering, blue-black skin is revealed to me. On instinct, I lean forward and bare my tongue, dragging it from the point just beneath his sternum up his chest and across one small, flat nipple. His breath hisses through his teeth.

"Ah, Tiani."

"You can call me Tee," I murmur as I trail my tongue across to the other side of his chest. I swirl it around his nipple until it hardens against my tongue. Something bumps my stomach, and I flinch back, my head dropping down as his dick swells between us.

"Tee, do I have your permission—"

"Yes, fuck me." I'm impatient. The desire to have him filling me is making me shake. No, it's making *him* shake. Beneath my hands, his skin vibrates. He follows my eyes to his arms where the skin tremors over his muscles.

"It is the *leht*. I need you," he groans as he nuzzles his nose into my low fro. It's such a sweet gesture that I immediate pull away. What we're doing isn't about sweet gestures. It's something else. It's lust. Obviously, we're both horny. There's no reason to reject good sex, but that's all it is.

"Hurry," I whisper, moving from his embrace and turning to face the window behind me. I drag the pajama shorts I'm wearing down my hips until they drop to my feet. Then I reach between my legs and pull my panties to the side, stretching the fabric up and over one of my ass cheeks as best I can to keep it out of the way.

"Tiani, turn back to me."

"No." I turned away for a reason. Being face to face with Bati makes me feel too many things I shouldn't be feeling. It confuses me. I don't want to be confused about this.

When he doesn't move, I spread my legs and reach between them, pushing my fingers through the dripping folds of my pussy. I lean down so that he has a clear view and sink two fingers up into my passage.

"Fuck, Bati, I'm so wet. Hurry."

BATI

I couldn't keep myself from giving Tiani what she's asking for even if I wanted to. Just the sight of her long, slim fingers disappearing into the wet, swollen cave of her pussy has me nearly releasing onto the pantry floor.

But I don't like it. I don't like how she's still holding herself away from me. Last night when we joined, I thought perhaps that she faced away from me to heighten her pleasure, but I am beginning to suspect that this is just another way of distancing herself from me. And while the sight of her full, round bottom is enough to bring me to my knees, I would see her face when I please her. I would witness her pleasure.

However, it appears I am not strong enough to resist the temptation that she offers because the moment my eyes fix on her glistening pussy, I have to be there, surrounded by her tight warmth.

"Bati," her plea is a needy moan. I waste no more time. I yank down my loose pants and step behind her. My cock is hard as stone and aimed straight at the slit that hides my new favorite place. I let the tip kiss her lips and suck in a breath as I'm seared by the heat of her pussy. It's too much.

I push forward, slipping past her lips and pressing into the tight warmth. We both moan loudly, and I brace a hand at her shoulder as I continue to feed my cock into her, persisting against the natural resistance of her body, observing as each inch is welcomed into her.

"Don't stop, Bati."

"I will not," I grind out because I have no intention to unless she says so. She's tight, and I don't miss the slight shift in her hips as I ascend through the quivering tissues of her passage. Her pleasure and arousal are so thick in the air that I open my mouth to catch it on my tongue before giving my hips one final thrust and seating myself completely inside of her.

"Ugh!" Her breathy little grunt as she takes the full length of my cock calls to some primal part of me. I flare with pride that she is able to take me so well. My eyes fall to the place where we're joined. The mouth of her pussy is stretched wide around me.

"My *lehti*." She has asked me not to call her this, but I take the liberty in this moment. She is too beautiful, too perfect for me not to acknowledge the *leht* that binds us.

I ease slowly out of her, my skin shaking with the effort, and then push back inside, savoring every drag of my cock through her softness. Tiani wiggles her hips, grinding her bottom into my pelvis.

"No, too slow. Faster. Harder."

I give her what she wants. I pull more quickly from her and when I reach the tip, I slam forward, seating myself with Lyqa speed. She gasps, raising up to her toes, and grips the edge of the window.

"Too much?"

"No, don't stop."

I don't. I give her all of me, thrusting into her over and over, pulling her back onto my cock as she moans and gasps. Her body clamps around me as she gets closer to her release. My own release hovers at the edge of my pleasure, a sharp almost painful sensation. I thrust faster, my hips a blur, but it stays just out of my reach. Tiani moans loudly beneath me, and suddenly I need to see her face. I need to kiss her beautiful mouth and look into the soft, black pools of her eyes.

I still my hips and step away from her, letting my cock slide from the slick cocoon of her pussy. As I hope, she gasps at the loss and spins around to face me. I lift her to my chest. Her legs go around my waist automatically, and I slide back inside of her in one, smooth thrust.

"Oh, god." Her breathy little prayer is sweet in my face. Earlier when we kissed, her mouth tasted of an Earth fruit called orange. It was fragrant and delicious, and I want to taste it again.

"I would see you come around my cock, my *lehti*." I slam my mouth down on hers and sweep my tongue in the moment she opens for me. At the same moment, I angle my hips up and lift her before bringing her down hard onto my length.

Her arms tighten around my neck, and the hard plates of her knees dig into my waist as she begins to spasm under the force of her orgasm. I swallow her sharp cry and then pull away to witness her come undone.

She's so beautiful. The smooth, brown skin of her face is slicked over with sweat. Her full lips part wide on a throaty moan. I flick my tongue over the sharp point of her cheekbone and her eyes flutter open. The long, curled row of lashes reveal the moons of her eyes. I'm lost.

"You are mine, Tiani. Do you hear me?" I slam my hips up and she gasps but remains quiet.

"Tiani, you are mine. My *lehti,* my heart. And I am yours. Say it." Again, she gasps around the force of my thrust. She squeezes her lips together even as a longing so intense it makes my heart trip pours off of her. Why does she fight it? Why fight me when I would give her everything?

"Tiani, stop fighting it. Listen to our hearts. I am yours," I thrust again. "You are mine. This pussy was fashioned for me.

You were fashioned for me. Now say it."

Her eyes plead up at me. I give her what she asks for, so she will give me what I want. I grip her hips and lift her high then bring her down until our flesh slaps loudly in the small space. Her mouth drops open on a silent cry.

"Say it."

"I—"

"Say it."

"I'm yours."

It is not said with the surety I would like, but it is enough for now. And more than enough to send me over the edge. My release charges through me, and I'm defenseless to contain the nearly feral growl that erupts from my chest. I continue to jerk my hips up as my balls tighten and my seed erupts against Tiani's womb. I pulse inside of her for long, drawn out moments, my entire body flinching as I spurt out my release. With one last surge, I empty the last of my seed. A deep sigh erupts from my chest as I hold Tiani's pelvis to mine.

I can't move for several moments. My upper body crowds over hers, and I breathe slowly in an effort to regain myself. My knees are bent, chairing her body against mine. They shake with the effort to keep us both upright. Within my chest, my first heart thuds heavily from its efforts. I hear Tiani's heart just beneath it, a slightly softer beat to my own. I raise my head and look down at her.

"Are you okay, did I hurt you?"

"No, I'm fine." She shakes her head. Her eyes shift around the room, and her expression is worried. I wonder if I have again "weirded her out" with the amount of my release.

"I will not release inside of you next time. I see that it makes you uncomfortable." I lean down to press a kiss to her soft mouth. Her lips remain still beneath mine.

She clears her throat and turns her face to the side. "No, it's fine. This was nice. It was great, again. I just really need to get back to making breakfast."

She has pulled herself away from me again. Perhaps my insistence on her admission that she belongs to me was too much. Shame crowds my heart. I should not have forced her in such a way.

"Why are you embarrassed?"

My arms are pulsing a bright pink. At this moment, I wish Lyqa were like humans and better able to conceal our emotions.

"I should not have made you say that," I admit quietly. She stares at me but doesn't respond. "I would not coerce you into loving me. I do not understand why you fight what is between us, what I know we can both feel in our hearts, but I will wait for you. I will wait as long as it takes for you to accept me."

I smile to show my sincerity and pass my hand over her soft crown of curls, but she flinches away. Her brow shifts down into a hard scowl.

"Bati, move. Let me down."

I immediately release her, and my cock slips free of her body followed by a gush of semen. She jerks her panties back in place and snatches her shorts from the floor.

"Why do you have to do that?" she protests as she shoves her legs into the shorts. Her jerky movements make her lose balance, and I reach out to steady her as she tilts to the side. "I don't need your help!" she shouts as she pulls from my grasp. I step away, giving her the space she requires. All I'm getting from her is annoyance. Her heart patters with agitation.

"I did not mean to rush you, my *lehti*."

She spins on me, her eyes flashing with hurt, an emotion I am surprised to see. "You're not rushing me because there is nothing to rush. I thought we had an understanding. You're cool, but I'm not your fucking girlfriend or your goddamn boo or anything. Us fucking doesn't mean all that. Why do you have to be all extra? And stop—," she stabs her finger against my chest and I step back—"calling me fucking Lettie! My name is Tiani. Ugh!"

She pushes past me and out of the pantry, and I'm left standing alone. The cloud of arousal that filled the small space is now sour with her anger.

Chapter 4

TIANI

I feel kind of bad for snapping at Bati.

We're all sitting at my mother's long, dining room table, and I can tell by all the Lyqa eyes avoiding me that our little squabble didn't go unnoticed. It's awkward as hell. I probably look like the biggest jerk in the world.

I don't know why what he said frustrated me so bad. He's just doing too much. I swear, you give one virgin alien a little bit of ass, and he acts like we're bound for life.

I feel someone looking at me, and when I raise my head from where it's lowered nearly to my plate, Amina glares at me. Right. I promised I wouldn't fuck him again, and that I'd be nice. Maybe I am a meanie after all.

Kwarq clears his throat and wipes his mouth with his napkin. I realize for the first time how much he and Bati look alike. Aside from skin and eye color, they're identical. From the moment I met him, Kwarq has been kind and caring. The way he looks at my sister, like she's the most important person in the universe, makes even my apparently cold heart flutter.

"I must take Amina back to Lyqa for the birthing of our

young, but before we leave, I would extend an invitation to you, Ms. Bennet, LaShay, and Tiani to join us if you wish."

"Uh, hell yeah, I'm coming." LaShay announces, and both me and Amina roll our eyes. Even if they hadn't offered, Shay probably would have stowed away on their ship. The girl barely lives on the planet as it is, so going to Lyqa isn't a stretch for her. The oldest brother, Ah'dan, fails at containing a groan after Shay's announcement. After a few days of them being with us, it's not a secret she annoys him. At least as much as any Lyqa can be annoyed.

Kwarq says something softly in Lyqa, and Ah'dan throws his hands up, issuing a short response back.

Amina glances between the two of them.

"Why are you telling him to be nice? Why aren't you being nice, Ah'dan?"

I forgot that my sister has been given some kind of translation device. She scowls between her husband and his brother, triggering Kwarq to narrow his eyes on Ah'dan. Surprisingly, when Ah'dan's eyes shift to Amina, they soften.

"I am sorry, my *sa'aih*. I spoke in jest. I did not mean any offense."

"I can come another time," LaShay mumbles.

"No, you can come now. Ignore him. He's always an ass," Amina says back, and Shay beams. She probably still would have stowed away.

"Mom, do you want to come for a while? It may be a good vacation."

"Sure," she says before scooping a forkful of eggs into her mouth. My eyes go wide at the same time as my sisters'.

"Are you serious?" I ask, and she shrugs her shoulders.

"Why not? It's not like something is going to eat me there. They're all vegetarians."

"Oh, okay," Amina stutters out and then shrugs, too. I don't think any of us were expecting her to agree. Of course, since I'm the last holdout, all eyes shift to me.

"You are also welcome to join us, Tiani. As is your son."

Several pairs of Lyqa eyes widen. Across the table on the opposite end, Bati's head snaps up. My heart stutters again. It's like someone is trying to start a lawnmower in my chest.

"You have young?" His voice sounds strangled. I slowly turn my head until I meet his shocked gaze.

"I have a son, yes," I reply and shift my eyes away.

"You are partnered already?" Bati's gaze is fixed on me.

"You mean, am I married?"

He slowly nods his head. He almost looks afraid of what I might say.

"Not anymore."

His face relaxes, and he smiles. I'm caught off guard by the brilliance of it. He looks so genuinely happy that I have to freeze the muscles in my face to stop myself from smiling back.

"So, you will come? And bring your son?"

I stall. Bati looks at me expectantly, and I don't know what to do. If I agree to come, will he think that means we're together or something?

"No," I return evenly and look away before his smile drops. I feel it though. An inexplicable wave of sadness crowds me, and I wish I could take it back.

Amina looks like she wants to jump across the table and strangle me. Her mouth is tight as she shakes her head back and forth. I look away, but my eyes immediately fall on Kwarq who's sitting next to her. His mouth is curved in a sad little smile that looks so much like it could be on Bati's face that I turn away from him, too.

"Why did you do that?"

I don't look up from where I'm folding one of my son's shirts. "Do what? I don't want to go."

"Yeah, but the way you said it. It was kind of rude." LaShay walks from the door to sit at the edge of my bed. She's about an inch from where me and Bati tackled each other last night. I try my best to focus on something else.

"How is it rude to say no?" I don't need her to tell me. I was a jerk.

"The same way it's rude to tell someone they're dusty. He was obviously excited that you might come. You could have clarified, at least."

I drop the shirt I'm holding and turn to her. "Why do I need to clarify anything to him?"

Shay's nose turns up in a classic stank face. "Stop being so fucking nasty, Tee. We get it. Your stupid husband left you alone to raise your son, so you don't trust no fucking body anymore. But seriously, he's been nothing but nice and respectful to you, and his family has, too. Did it ever occur to you that you just embarrassed the fuck out of him?"

The guilt I've been trying to hold back since I opened my mouth rushes over me. I definitely could have rejected their offer in a nicer way.

"Shit. Ugh!" I cover my face. I hate crying, but I kind of want to cry. I don't know why I'm feeling like this all of a sudden. No, I do know why, and he's bluish-black and tall and fine and probably downstairs pulsing bright pink.

BATI

I ignore the ache in my first heart. Tiani is human. I cannot expect the *leht* to anticipate the emotional inclinations of humans. To anticipate that she may not share the same attachment to me. I warned my brother of this when he first recognized his *lehti*. I should have heeded this warning as well.

My mother keeps trying to catch my gaze, but I avoid it. I

don't want to witness her sorrow. She is a feeler, and since I cannot easily hide my emotions from her, I would rather not see how she reacts to them.

"Um, Bati, can I talk to you for a minute?"

I look up to find Tiani standing in front of me. Immediately, that pull resumes. Her voice flows over me, and the ache in my heart eases just a bit.

"Of course, Tiani."

I stand and follow her into the small hallway beyond the living room. I can smell her regret as she walks ahead of me. When she stops and turns to face me, guilt is a thick cloud between us.

"I'm sorry I snapped at you earlier, and I'm sorry I was so rude when you asked me to come to Lyqa. You didn't deserve that."

She is so beautiful. Like Amina, she is brown, but slightly lighter. Her short, dark hair curls into perfect ringlets about her head. The black eyes that stare up at me are heavy with sorrow. I cannot stop myself from smoothing a hand over her face. Her eyes close briefly before blinking open. She eases her face into my touch, and I lower my hand, aware that I have touched her without her permission.

"You do not have to apologize to me, Tiani. You were very clear from our initial interactions that you did not desire any attachment to me. I should not have pressed my suit."

"No, I mean. It's okay. I mean, I do like you. It's just—," she pauses and frustration colors her scent. I do not like her agitated on my behalf.

"It is okay, Tiani," I tell her, and my heart jerks with a sharp pain. "I cannot fault you for not feeling the same way I do. You have made your wishes clear, and I will bother you with my affection no longer." I do not wait for her to respond. I return to the living room and prepare to leave my *lehti*.

* * *

Kwarq, Amina, LaShay, and Ms. Bennet are waiting when I return. Tiani comes into the room behind me and the feel of her at my back is crushing. I need to be away from her, even as I want to be as close to her as possible.

"LaShay, Ms. Bennet, if you wish, I can carry these to the car for you." I smile and wait until they hold their bags out before taking them. I turn to the door and close my hand over the handle.

"Bati—" Tiani's voice is small behind me. It tears at my already aching heart. I push the sensation away. She is not mine. She has made it clear she does not wish to be with me. I smile sadly to myself as I realize that the first words I ever heard spoken of Tiani were advice I should have heeded after all.

"Whatever it is you think is between the two of you means more to you than it does to Tee. The sooner you can realize that, the sooner you can get on with your life and find a young woman who wants to be with you. Tee ain't it."

Aside from the fact that there is no other woman for me, the main point of her mother's warning is true. Tee—as she so wisely tried to tell me—ain't it.

"It was a pleasure to meet you, Tiani. I wish you well."

I step out onto the porch and carry the bags to Kwarq's vehicle. I press the button and the lid to the rear storage space opens.

I drop the bags inside, wishing I could rip my heart out and toss it inside as well. At least, I realize, the echo of our hearts is now so soft that I can ignore it if I try very hard.

"Don't go after it, let it roll back, KJ!"

My attention is drawn to the right where an older human woman rushes across the grass toward me. The look on her face shifts quickly from admonishment to panic before she starts to sprint toward the street, her arm outstretched as a shrill scream issues from her throat.

Her fear is pungent. It rushes over me, and I turn to the source just in time to see a small boy appear from between two parked vehicles. His head is bent low, tiny fingers outstretch as he pursues a small, orange ball. It rolls, just out of his reach, and the child scrambles after it, unaware of the panicked woman rushing after him.

Her panic is justified. A large, black vehicle, nearly two times the size of Kwarq's small car, barrels down the street. Music sounds loudly from the open window, drowning out the woman's cries. I do not have to be human to know that when the vehicle hits this child, his life will be extinguished.

It is nearly upon him. The woman has only just made it to the curb, but she is too slow. She trips, falling forward and catching herself with one hand. The other still reaches for the boy, who, finally having caught the ball, turns back with a confused look at the woman's panic.

My heart lurches. Not in fear, with something else. Something instinctual and vibrant. The car—no, truck, my language implant supplies the word—bears down on him, and I know that any harm to this boy would result in a pain greater than I could withstand.

I move forward without thinking, uncaring that my speed is unnatural in this place. Uncaring that the woman gasps as I blur past her. The startled thump of her heart barely reaches my ears. I'm looking at the boy. His small, brown face finally shows recognition of the danger that's about to overcome him, and he flinches away, tucking his head into his shoulder.

I reach him just as the truck gets close enough that the tail of the boy's flapping shirt brushes the front of the bumper. I wrap my arms around him, crouching low to shield him with my torso. He's so small that he nearly disappears against me. I'm glad. I'm moving too fast to stop myself before the truck hits us, but I hope that I will at least take the brunt of it. I scoop him from the ground and spin around in a circle, trying my best to evade the vehicle. I nearly make it, but just as I spin away, a sharp pain burns through my side where the truck catches me at my lower back. I drop to one knee, unable for a moment to breathe. My vision goes blurry. As I lose consciousness, I feel out to the boy. He smells afraid, but not in pain. I'm glad because that means he is unharmed and merely startled.

The thought enters my mind that I must accept that I will never have young. But if I am to die, this moment is what I imagine fatherhood to be. And even though I do not know this little boy, my spirit sings with an inexplicable love for him. That was the feeling in my heart. That lurch. It was amazing. Almost as amazing as the love I have for Tiani. I smile to myself. If I am to die, I am glad I was able to know this kind of love, even if it was just in my own heart. I close my eyes to this thought right before I hear the distinct sound of Tiani scream.

Chapter 5

TIANI

I can't make it down the stairs quick enough. I nearly fall when I trip over my feet on the last step, but I stumble through it and make a dash for the spot where Bati's fallen beside the curb.

He was fast. So fast that he was no more than a bluish-black blur as he sped toward the truck. I'd followed him out, hoping to apologize. Hoping to say something to him before he left. To let him know that maybe what happened between us wasn't as meaningless as I let on, but then I saw the truck. It was Tre', the fucker from next door. Tre's cool, but he doesn't understand the meaning of *there are kids on this block.* I've yelled at him countless times to slow the hell down when he's driving down our street, but he doesn't listen.

Tre's truck is still barreling down the street as I run across the grass and drop to my knees beside Bati. My heart thumps so hard I can barely breathe. He's so still. The back of his shirt is torn where the truck clipped him. Beneath it, the skin is scrapped and raw. A clear luminescent fluid oozes from beneath the broken flesh.

I'm worried about Bati, but I'm more worried about what

we're going to find when we turn him over. My urge is to push him aside, but I stop myself. If he's hurt, it may do more damage.

"*Sa'aih,* please move aside. Let us see that he is unharmed."

I turn terrified eyes on Kwarq, as he leans down beside me. His face is a mask of sympathy, but beneath it is a worry so intense that I can feel it.

I scoot over. He and Ah'dan take hold of Bati's shoulders and legs and flip him carefully onto his back. Immediately, the breath that's been burning through my chest whooshes out as the tiny, curled up form of my son becomes visible.

He was shielded in the cocoon of Bati's body. He looks shook, but otherwise okay. The moment Bati is moved, he jumps from the ground into my arms.

"Mommy!"

"KJ, oh my god. Are you okay?" I squeeze his arms and legs. I run my hands down his little body, making sure everything is alright. He tolerates my frantic inspection with quiet unease. I know I look crazed.

"My ball went into the street." KJ's chin wobbles as he misinterprets my expression as anger. I'm not angry. I'm terrified.

"I know, baby. Consider this me yelling at you for following your ball into the street. I don't know how any times I told you never to do that."

He's fine. I pull him into a hug and squeeze tight. His arms come around my neck.

"Sorry, mommy."

"That's okay, baby. Go to Auntie Shay. I have to see if my friend is okay."

I pass him off to my sister, who's standing behind me looking about as ready to cry as KJ. Shay loves these Lyqa. It didn't take much for her to start thinking of them as her own. At the moment, I understand.

I move next to Kwarq. Bati's still unconscious, and I want to shake him and make him open those ocean blue eyes for me.

"Is he okay?"

I assume because his family isn't freaking the hell out that he's not dead. At least I hope he's not dead. Just the thought makes me queasy.

"He is okay. He has just been stunned." Quth, their father, runs his arm over Bati's back and abdomen then taps a slim metal bracelet at his wrist. A projection of some kind beams a few inches above it. "There is no damage. He will recover, but we should get him inside. People have come out of their homes to observe."

I glance around. People are standing on their porches. Of course, they are. Black folks aren't going to miss a chance to see some drama.

Behind us, my mother tries to calm my ex-husband's mother. She was dropping KJ off after he spent the night with her.

"Did you see that boy run?" There's no mistaking the shock in her voice.

"I know, Annette. He's some kind of track star. Good thing, too." My mother steers Annette away as the other woman tries to resist.

"That was not normal!" she protests.

"Annette, you better get on home and clean those scrapped knees. You're gonna scar." My mother gently pushes her off in the direction of her house up the street. Annette stumbles away but continues to look back in confusion.

"Let's go on and get this boy inside." My mother nudges her head in the direction of the gathering crowd of neighbors. Kwarq and Ah'dan lift Bati between them and carry him into the house.

* * *

"You're sure he's okay? Why hasn't he woken up, yet?" I'm dogging their heels. Bati's mother is right beside me. Her eyes, which are bright and blue like Bati's, shine with tears. They're made of the same luminescent fluid that seeped from the wound in Bati's back.

"I am not sure, my *dahnai*. I must examine him further," Quth returns somewhat impatiently. "He may just be stunned. Sleep is a natural defense of the Lyqa body. Any severe trauma will often result in a resting period to allow for recovery."

"He's in a coma?" My voice rises in panic.

"It's not a coma, Tee. Get back. He wouldn't even be out there if it weren't for you."

I turn to a glaring Amina. I can't deny that her words sting my already stinging heart. She pushes past me and rushes to open the door to her room. Kwarq and Ah'dan carry Bati in and gently deposit him on the bed.

Kwarq turns to my sister and frowns. It's the first time I've ever seen him look at her with anything but complete adoration.

"We are happy that he was outside. Imagine what would have happened to our *dah'san* if he had not been. You are too harsh with her." He looks to me. "It is the pregnancy. Her emotions are unstable. Please forgive her."

When he turns a pointed look on Amina, she stares back at him for a second before sighing heavily and walking over to me.

"Fine! *Ma'h qitah*, Tee," she drags out like it's the last thing she wants to say. She wraps her hands around my waist and squeezes me as best she can with her belly. I can only stare down at her. She looks like she did when we were kids and my mother made her apologize to me. "I shouldn't have said that to you, blah blah blah."

She lets me go and steps away before stabbing her finger at

me defiantly.

"You better be happy he was rescuing K or else I would *never* talk to you again!" She huffs and storms off. When I turn my confusion on Kwarq, he rolls his eyes.

"She is doing the most," he says in his weird Lyqa accent and turns back to his brother.

Bati's face is so still against the pillow. I lingered outside the door to my sister's room like a weirdo until his mother finally came into the hall and told me to come in. I thought she'd be mad at me for treating her son like shit, but she's been perfectly nice. Just like Bati. Just like this whole Lyqa family. Guilt eats at me. I really am rotten.

"Is he going to wake up soon?"

"He will wake when his body has contained the trauma. This is not unexpected," his father replies gently, but he looks worried. Bati's mother, too, looks terrified. Her eyes are puffy from crying.

I can't stop myself from reaching out a hand to smooth it over his cap of tight red curls. He's so strange looking, but still so handsome. I've spent a lot of time pretending I don't want to look at him, mostly so he wouldn't see how much I really want to look at him, but now that I have the chance, I can't look away.

All I can think about is how light my heart is when he's around. Something I was all too happy to ignore earlier today, but now it feels like the most urgent thing in the world. I want to hold him. I want to slide into the bed beside him and rub over all of his smooth, warm skin. I want—him.

I'm an idiot. My whole life, I've been dodging no good ass dudes, and the moment I find someone who looks at me like I'm the best thing since sliced bread, I send him packing back to his planet. What the hell was I thinking?

I tell myself that when he wakes up, I'm gonna take it back.

Maybe seeing where this whole Lyqa lust thing can go isn't such a bad idea.

BATI

I smell Tiani. She's a light flowery scent that makes my heart thump with excitement. I think for a moment that I may have dreamt her rejection. Perhaps she is here with me now in this too small bed, and everything is as it should be.

The lingering smell is cut sharply by my mother's worry. Ah, yes. The boy. The truck. The moment I believed myself to be dying. That wonderful contentment that filled my heart. But I am not dead. The soft sounds of my mother's weeping tear at my spirit, and I will my eyes to open, so that I may put her mind at ease.

"I am well, mother." I say this in Lyqa, and a second later, the sweet cloud of her fragrance, a smell I have found comfort in since the day I was born, surrounds me.

"*Dahni*, you nearly killed me."

She does not speak in metaphor. As her child, we share the *lehti'an*. My death would have weakened her spirit. It is not uncommon for Lyqa mothers to follow their dead children if the grief is too intense.

"I am sorry, mother." I'm still staring at the dark insides of my lids. I crack my eyes open. Everything above me is obscured by the large mass of my mother's curling hair. I open my mouth to speak but only end up taking in a mouthful of the soft strands.

"*Lehti*, let our son breathe. Choking him to death now that he is conscious will not do any good."

My mother raises her head, and her large, blue eyes—eyes like my own—are swollen and red. Behind her, my father brushes at his own eyes before leaning down to place a kiss on my head.

"I'm glad that you are okay. I don't think I would have been able to bear it if we lost you."

I take hold of his hand and squeeze. "I am well father, do not worry."

"You talk funny."

I turn my head to the side, and I'm met by the scrunched-up face of the boy from the street. Large round eyes framed with tightly curled lashes stare down at me. Something about them is familiar. His round, brown face is plump the way babies' faces are. Other than that, he is a scrawny little thing. It is quite adorable.

He's holding a small toy vehicle, not unlike the one that nearly took his life, and I'm strangely comforted by the idea that he is shielded from the trauma of his experience by such innocence. I am also overcome by the same sensation of love that I felt outside. It makes me sit up, wincing at the pain in my side, before I reach out to lift him and pull him into my lap.

I cradle him against my chest, just needing to reassure myself he is unharmed. He holds himself rigidly in my arms, but allows me hold him for a few moments. I'm careful not to squeeze him too tight. He is much smaller than Lyqa children.

"Why are you hugging me?"

I pull away, remembering again that such displays of affection are awkward among humans. I set him back from me and rub my hand playfully over his head, the way my father did to me when I was young.

"I apologize for touching you without your permission, KJ. You scared me very badly outside, and I would know that you are unharmed."

"What's unharmed mean?"

I chuckle.

"It means not hurt."

"Oh," he's turning the car over in his hands, but staring

closely at my face. Suddenly, his eyes narrow, and it's a very familiar gesture. "How do you know my name?"

"The woman you were with called it out. I am sure you have already been told, but it is always best to allow a toy to come back to you rather than pursue it into oncoming traffic."

"Huh?" His mouth turns up in a confused smile, and I find myself smiling back.

"Do not chase your ball into the street."

"Oh, my mommy already yelled at me," he sighs out in a small voice. I cannot tell his age, but he is very intelligent. I feel a sense of pride in this fact. Although, I don't know why.

"Is your mother also unharmed? I saw that she fell."

The boy's face scrunches up again, and I'm once more hit with the sense of familiar. "That was my Grammy Spence. Mommy is downstairs with my aunts, my new uncles, and my other grandma."

Ah, of course. I look up to my parents in question and they smile. This is Tiani's son. I would have realized it, eventually. There is no other reason that my connection to him would be so strong. The same *leht* that has bound me to his mother has also connected me to him. I hear his little heartbeat. A soft patter beneath mine.

"Is there damage? Can I stand?" My father, who was once a healer, shakes his head.

"I have scanned you. There is no internal damage. Some bruising. You are quick, my *dahni*. I am thankful for that."

"Your name is Danny?"

I turn back to the boy. He moves closer, settling against my arm. He lifts his hand and pokes at my cheek as if trying determine if I am real. I let him.

"No, *dahni* means 'son'."

"This is your dad?" He points to my father who smiles warmly.

"He is."

"And that's your mommy?" He shifts his little finger to my mother, and she smiles widely. I know both of my parents have probably already begun to think of him as their grandchild.

"She is."

He leans away and looks up at me.

"Do you know my mommy?"

I smile. "I do."

"Are you her friend?"

I think back to the moment when Tiani told me that we meant nothing to each other, and that slight ache returns to my chest. However, I force my smile to stay in place.

"I am not a friend of your mother's, but I am good friends with your Aunt Amina," I tell him instead. I would not lie. Not even to a child.

"KJ, where are you?"

Tiani's voice carries through the open door a second before she appears there. She looks first at me, and immediately her expression shifts. She smells anxious. I'm struck with the realization that she has most likely been filled with guilt that I was hurt. I don't like it. She has nothing to be guilty about, and I would get hit by a thousand trucks to ensure the safety of her son.

KJ jumps and scrambles away, slipping out into the hall. Tiani looks at me for another moment. Her anxiety shifts to something very close to warmth. She appears to want to speak. But, instead, she turns and leaves, closing the door after her.

It takes me a while to get the strength to rise from the small bed. My brothers burst into the room after Tiani leaves, both awash with relief. My and Kwarq's twin second hearts trip into rhythm the moment he walks into the door, and his agony washes over me.

"I am okay. Do not worry."

Ah'dan follows him in, making a fuss about me being clumsy before embracing me with a deep sigh. He only stays for a moment then he ushers our parents out, aware that Kwarq and I require a moment alone. The bond between Lyqa twins is almost as strong as the *leht*.

"You saved her son," Kwarq acknowledges when we are alone.

"It was the *leht*. I would have tried to save him anyway, but the feeling inside of me, the instinct to protect him was so strong, I felt like it took over. Like I was outside of myself, looking in."

My brother nods in understanding. "I know how you describe. So, what will you do?" he asks after a moment. I don't have to question what he means, but I do not know if anything has changed that would allow me to stay. I'm sure Tiani is grateful, but that is not what I want. I want her love. Having met KJ, it is an even more difficult realization that I am not only letting go of a *lehti* but also of a son.

"I would not let guilt change her mind. I will still go."

Kwarq looks as if this is the response he was expecting. A twinge of sadness rolls off him, and I grip his shoulder in comfort.

"Do not be sad for me, brother."

"I would have you know the contentment of the *leht*. I would have you feel the love that I have with Amina."

"I know, but it is not meant to be. It's okay. Sometimes it's this way." I repeat this to myself as I let him help me stand. Perhaps if I tell myself this enough, it will one day be true.

Chapter 6

TIANI

The moment Bati turns the corner into the living room, I jump to my feet. I've been rehearsing what I want to say since I ran out of his room like a coward. Fearful the words will evade me again, I rush to speak.

"Bati, thank you so mu—"

I move toward him, but he stops me with a raised hand. It feels like rejection.

"You do not need to thank me, Tiani. I am only glad that I was here to offer assistance," he doesn't look at me. He stares down at my son, who's playing with a pile of toy cars on the floor. He kneels down and rubs his hand over KJ's hair, and I have to close my eyes around the pain that surges through me at the thought of what probably would have happened if he hadn't been there.

Amina said she never would have talked to me again if something happened to Bati, but I'm sure I never would have talked to myself. I want to hug him. I want to feel for myself that he is okay, but he held his hand up to me. He totally gave me the Lyqa hand.

"It was nice to meet you, my *dahni*. Promise me that you

will be very careful while playing in the future." He surprises me by leaning in to press a kiss to the top of KJ's head. He pulls back to rise, but KJ hops to his feet and hurls himself against Bati, his little arms going around Bati's neck and squeezing tight.

"Thanks for not letting me get hit by a car," KJ mumbles. I'm unsure of what to do. Bati's eyes flick up to me for a split second, and I think I see sadness there. He wraps his arms around my son in a gentle hug and then eases him away.

"You are a very clever boy. Be happy and try not to give your mother a hard time."

KJ nods and drops back to the ground like this display of closeness with Bati was the most normal thing in the world.

Bati rises from his knees, grimacing as he straightens his back. He got hit by a truck for my son. He could have died, and I get the impression he would have been okay with that if it meant KJ was okay. That urge to touch him, to kiss him, is so strong. But he still hasn't looked at me, and I don't think that's by accident.

"Are you sure you're okay?"

It's such a stupid question. He got hit by a truck. I don't know Lyqa anatomy, but I imagine that anyone getting hit by a truck wouldn't be one hundred percent okay. He looks a little worse for wear. His face is drawn as if he's in pain, and he keeps pressing a hand to his lower back.

"I am well, Tiani. Do not trouble yourself with concern for me." He turns away from me to face his family. He's not so subtly telling me to kick rocks. I can't blame him.

"Are we ready to depart?" he asks his brothers, and my chest twinges painfully. I don't want him to go, but I can't get my mouth to form the words to ask him to stay. And anyway, what would him staying do? Give me a chance to take back being a jerk to him? Then what? He'll have to leave eventually.

"Amina is in the middle of a hunger. As soon as she has had her fill, we will go to the pods. It should not be long. She is nearing her birthing. She is insatiable."

Kwarq looks away, and a deep blush pulses his golden skin. Since my sister has been home, she's basically spent her time shoveling food into her mouth and shoving her tongue down her husband's throat. Apparently, Lyqa pregnancy makes her hungry and horny. At least she has an excuse. I don't know what made me act the way I did with Bati. I mean, obviously, he's fine. It didn't take much for me to want him. And now he won't even look at me.

"I'll go check if she's finished," I mumble and scurry out of the room like the little monster I am.

"You're an asshole, you know that?"

Amina halts the fork holding a large spool of spaghetti at her mouth only long enough to get her words out and then she shovels it in. Her eyes close in satisfaction.

"Mm!" She chews slowly, lapping up the bits of sauce around her mouth. It's kind of gross. No one should enjoy food as much as she is right now.

"Since when do you like spaghetti?" When we were kids, our mother couldn't get her to touch the stuff. She said it looked like worms.

I sit across from her and pick up a slice of garlic bread from a plate in the middle of the table. Mina's eyes shoot over to me on a scowl.

"Since fifteen minutes ago," she mumbles around the fork that can't get the sauce-soaked noodles into her mouth quick enough.

"Hm, that's weird," I return, honestly. This whole Lyqa business didn't take long to become a regular thing in our weird ass family, but Amina eating an entire pot of spaghetti is not something I'll ever get used to. I'm getting a stomach ache just watching her.

"You're an asshole," she says again. Little bits of spaghetti fly out of her mouth when she talks. Her eyes stay glued to the fragments of noodle for a second too long for it not to be weird.

"I know." I do.

"He saved KJ." She pauses for real, even though her hand wavers with the urge to bring it to her mouth.

"I know." I will never forget the moment Kwarq rolled Bati's limp body over to reveal a scared but alive KJ wrapped in his arms. I will also never forget how hard my heart was beating until Kwarq confirmed that Bati was still alive.

"He cares about you, Tee."

"I know," I admit again. "This whole thing just threw me off. I like him, I do. I wasn't expecting to feel that way, you know."

"Tee, come with us. Hang out on Lyqa. Get to know him."

I really want to say yes. "I don't know about taking my son to an alien planet," I return instead. It's not a complete cop out.

"Ugh, I hate when you act like this." Amina sneers and looks away from me. She must be over her hunger because she drops the fork to the plate with a clatter and pushes everything across the table to the other side.

"Like what?"

"Like you don't want to do anything."

"Just cause I don't want to go to an alien planet with you and your tall ass boyfriend?"

"First, he's my husband. And, no, cause you act like there's a real reason for you not to go. There's nothing to be afraid of. It's safe there. Probably safer than it is here. This is an opportunity of a lifetime. You're only saying no to be ornery."

Amina is mad. Like big mad. She snatches up the plate from the other side of the table and rushes it over to the trash like it's contaminated, her head pulled back on her neck, her face a grimace. I stand and follow her to the sink where she's rinsing off the plate. I wrap my arms around her from the back, rocking her back and forth playfully.

"Did you just call me ornery?"

"Yup."

"What am I, eighty?"

"You act eighty. You're the only person I know who would get a chance to go to another planet and say no."

"So, now, I'm a bad person because I'm suspect about dragging my son off to a whole 'nother alien fucking planet? Can't I just be a good parent? Damn."

Amina turns to me, and her face is a blank mask of gtfoh.

"Seriously? That's what you're going to go with? 'I'm trying to be a good parent'? Your son would like officially be a fucking astronaut, okay? He'd be fucking Jean-Luc Picard. He'd be Captain James T. Kirk. He'd be fucking Spock."

"Spock is a Vulcan," I return dryly, and she huffs out a lungful of air and rolls her eyes.

"Then he'd be goddamn Geordi La Forge. You know what the hell I mean. Either way, he's four. Nothing's going to happen there, and if worse comes to worst, the Lyqa can do that *Men in Black* mind erase thing on him, and he'll be fine."

I stare at my sister. Five minutes ago, I wasn't even considering going to Lyqa, and now I am, mostly because of Bati. And the chance for KJ to be Geordi fucking La Forge. Amina always knows just what to say to make me consider something, so I shouldn't be surprised when I hear myself saying:

"Fine, but only because you said we can get there and back in the blink of an eye. If this was some epic, stasis necessary journey through space, you and that fine Lyqa could kiss my ass. I can always dress KJ up as Geordi for Halloween."

* * *

"Tiani said she'd come!" My shoulder's flinch when Amina squeals this out as we walk back into the living room. She's really happy about this. Like really happy. She rushes over to Kwarq and takes his hands before jumping awkwardly up and down with what can only be described as giddy delight. He smiles down patiently at her as she dances her rollie little self around the hallway. I frown at this strange display of excitement.

"It is the babies. All of her emotions are heightened," Kwarq says with an apologetic shrug.

Right. Creepy Lyqa pregnancy. Amina's little hallway celebration is the weirdest thing ever, and I've just agreed to go to a planet with a bunch of these people. Granted they are nice. They're probably the nicest people I've ever met. It wouldn't be too bad for KJ to be around a bunch of nice people. And since Amina has assured me that nothing will try to eat him, I guess I can do this.

"K, come here, baby."

My son, who is still playing with his cars on the floor, gets up and walks over to me. This kid hasn't even batted an eye at the five ginormous aliens in our house. I guess when you're as little as he is, these differences don't matter. Maybe that's a good lesson to learn at his age.

I bend down and pull him against me. I've been trying not to make a big deal about his whole brush with death. Once he was okay, he carried on as usual, so I resisted the urge to hold on to him for dear life like I want to. But now that he's in my arms, I can't help but lean in to smell his sweet little cap of curls. My baby. I don't know what I would have done if he'd been hurt.

With the group of Lyqa standing behind him, it's almost like he has his own personal bodyguards. I wouldn't bet my life on a lot of stuff, but I'd bet my life that they won't let anything happen to him on Lyqa.

"Hey, buddy. We're going to take a trip. What do you think about that?"

The moment I say 'trip' KJ looks up from his toy car with wide excited eyes. Then he turns and points a finger up at Bati.

"Is he coming?"

I follow his hand. Bati looks down at KJ, but not at me. I gently take hold of his wrist and bring it down to his side. I'm really going to have to teach this kid that it's rude to point.

"Uh, yeah, he's coming."

KJ smiles. "Good, I like him. He's my friend." He bounces out of my arms and over to Bati before taking the Lyqa's large blue-black hand in his own. He smiles up at his rescuer and does his own giddy little dance, which triggers a round of chuckles from the others.

I ease back to my feet and clasp my hands in front of me, sending up a silent prayer that this not be the biggest mistake of my life.

"Well, I guess I better go pack."

BATI

It takes all of me not to shout with joy when Tiani announces she and KJ are coming to Lyqa. I know she has only agreed to please her sister, but a small part of me hopes that perhaps she has come to feel differently toward me.

Something has changed. The edge of resistance I have felt from her since we met has lessened. She's still nervous, but the few times our gazes cross, she smiles tentatively. Even as my hope cultivates, I try not to put too much faith in it.

"How shall we divide our travelers?"Ah'dan's smile is mischievous.

He and Kwarq returned to Lyqa to exchange our transports for larger pods. The new pods can each hold five travelers, which I'm sure is no coincidence.

"Can I ride with you?"

Taini's sister LaShay steps forward and takes hold of Ah'dan's arm. He scowls down at her, but does not move away. I heard Amina scolding him to accommodate her. This is his attempt.

"If you must. Tiani, which would you like to take?"

"I want to ride with Bati!" KJ bounces away from his mother and grabs my hand. I smile down at him, but I'm sure to return my expression to a neutral one when I look at his mother.

"I do not mind keeping an eye on him if you would like to travel with Amina and your mother."

"Oh, I mean, I can ride with you guys. If that's okay."

She's nervous, and again that little bit of hope surges through me. The desire to sweep her up against me and kiss away all of her anxiety makes me root myself to the spot. It takes everything I have to turn back to Ah'dan.

"We four shall ride with you then."

His smile widens. I ignore it and lift KJ into the pod. The pod hovers several feet off the ground. It will be impossible for the humans to enter on their own.

Before I can assist her, LaShay launches herself over the edge of the opening and lands heavily on her stomach. A loud whoosh of air erupts from her mouth, followed by a cackle.

"Well that isn't what was supposed to happen," she mumbles and drops back to the ground, prepared to attempt again.

"Let me help you." Ah'dan's tone suggests he does not want to help at all. LaShay turns with a smile and raises her arms so he can grab her by the waist. His expression is neutral as he lifts her and settles her easily into the craft.

"Thanks, boo," she gives him a wink. Ah'dan shakes his

head.

"I do not know what that means."

"You will," she returns with another sly smile. It is obvious to everyone that she has developed some kind of affection for him. I hope she is not disappointed when she learns that Ah'dan has already been *leht*.

I expect Ah'dan to help Tiani in next, but he walks around the craft and climbs into the operator's seat, forcing me to assist my *lehti*.

I turn to find her watching me. That same nervous energy is vibrant between us.

"You don't have to help me. I can try to get in myself." She steps to move around me, and I cut her off, taking gentle hold of her waist.

"Do you think I would deny myself the opportunity to touch you?"

I don't know why I tell her this. Why I reveal myself in this way, but when her eyes flare with desire, and not annoyance as I expect, I flex my hands and pull her closer.

"Bati?"

"Yes, Tiani?"

"I—"

I wait. I do not know what she wants to say, but just being this close to her is enough for me. It has been less than five hours since we were together in the kitchen of her house, but it feels as if between that time and now, galaxies have come between us. I savor the moment of closeness.

She stares up at me. I am aware of everyone waiting in the craft behind us. When she continues to look at me without speaking, I lift her—she weighs nearly nothing—and settle her into the craft. I walk around to sit on the opposite side, across the aisle from her. As long as she is here, I will take advantage of her proximity and be as close to her as I can.

Chapter 7

TIANI

There's a reason I don't go on roller coasters. I hate that feeling. That moment of weightlessness. That second when your body defies gravity. Lyqa space travel might be quick, but I still have the urge to puke the second after Ah'dan warns us to close our eyes and blips us to Lyqa.

"Ugh." I press my eyes tighter shut and lean forward in my seat. My stomach rolls like little waves crest back and forth inside of it, and I swallow hard around the acidic taste of tomato that rises to the back of my throat.

"It will ease in a moment."

A large, warm hand rests gently over my back and begins to rub slow circles between my shoulder blades. A little jolt of excitement runs through me at the contact, and when I turn my head to peer at him, Bati's bright blue eyes are creased with concern.

"Mommy has a weak stomach," KJ supplies from the seat next to him. I tried to get him to sit next to me, but he insisted on sitting next to his new best friend. Apparently, if someone saves you from being hit by a car once, you forget the woman who pushed you out of her vagina.

"It would seem she does, but it is up to us with strong stomachs to help those with weaker ones." Bati moves his strokes lower on my back. The warmth and movement of his hand counters the rolling in my belly, and it actually starts to ease a bit.

After another moment, I clear my throat, take one final deep breath and sit up. Bati pulls his arm back across the short isle.

"Thank you," I mumble, more embarrassed than ever at how much of a jerk I was to him. He's really the sweetest guy I've ever met.

"Of course, Tiani." Those sparkly blues linger on my face for a moment before he turns to lean his head down to KJ and point out the window.

"This is my home. It is called Lyqa."

KJ braces his hands on the armrests of his seat and pushes himself up to peer over the edge of the window.

"Woooow!"

I haven't looked around yet, but KJ's wide eyed look of wonder, makes me turn my head to the square window to my right.

"Holy shit."

"Ooo, mommy, you cursed."

"Sorry, baby."

Holy shit. I'm on another planet.

Lyqa is beautiful. The ground below us is lush and green. Above us, the sky is a blanket of glittering stars. They twinkle in purples, pinks, and greens. A sea of precious stones—diamonds, emeralds, amethyst, sapphires. Like someone took a handful of pixie dust and tossed it into the sky.

About a hundred yards away, in the open night space, a vaporous swirl of smoke spreads into a large black hole. A second later, a pod appears from the gaping hole, bobbing, suspended in the bright night sky. It creeps slowly forward and drops behind a row of pods lined up before some kind of floating tollbooth.

"Do you see this shit, Tee!" LaShay's geeked voice sounds out behind me. I was starting to wonder if she was conscious back there, but apparently, she was just rendered speechless for a moment. That's shocking in itself.

"Ooo, Auntie Shay, you cursed."

Shay snorts out a laugh. "Boy, please, you might as well cover your ears now."

"Shay…" I warn.

"I'm only kidding, but you gotta admit that this shi—stuff—is pretty awesome. And to think, you weren't even going to come."

She's right. I would have been pissed if I had missed this. When I was kid, I used to lay out on our back patio and stare up at the sky, trying desperately to drown out the sounds of my parents yelling in the house, the boys yelling down the block, the occasional loud, suspicious pop. I would focus on the few stars that were visible in the sky and imagine being somewhere else. Anywhere else. Now, there's an entire world in front of me that I never could have imagined.

A giddy flutter replaces the queasy roll in my stomach. I'm on an alien planet. My son is Geordi LaForge and I'm fucking Nyota Uhura.

"You have a beautiful smile, Tiani."

My head swivels over to Bati. From across the short isle, his eyes sparkle enough to rival anything outside of the window.

"Thank you," I manage to push out on a nervous breath. I am smiling. Actually, I'm grinning like a cat. This is amazing. It's so great that I can't even pretend like being here with Bati doesn't make it better. It's almost like all of the nervousness I felt about being attracted to him has lifted away, and without thinking, I reach across the aisle and lay my hand over his, giving it a little squeeze. He jumps, his skin twitching beneath my palm.

"I'm so sorry about before." The shame at my behavior is so intense that it's no wonder I'm not pulsing bright pink. "I shouldn't have treated you like that. And thank you again for saving my son."

"My *lehti*, I have told you, you do not have to thank me, but I would save him every day if it meant you are happy."

That does it. Like a billion years of fucks that I've let go of come rushing back to me. My throat clogs around a ball of emotion, and before I know it, I'm pulling my hand back to cover my face as a rough sob jerks through my body.

"I'm sorry." This is what I mean to say, but it comes out as something else. Some strange warble of sound and snot. I try to take a deep breath, to stop whatever is happening, but I can't. It's coming up from my gut, like a pot boiling over. It burns its way up my throat. I can't believe I'm crying on a spaceship.

I hear Bati move next to me before I'm being lifted and settled into the cradle of his lap. He's warm and hard but there is a comfort here. I press into it, wrapping my arms around his middle and nestling my head into the space below his shoulder.

"I'm sorry," I whisper again. My throat is raw. I don't know how long I've been crying, but everything around us is quiet. I let myself believe for a moment that we're alone. That it's just the two of us. Me and Bati, chilling on a spaceship.

"Why is Mommy crying?"

KJ's worried little voice snaps me out of my moment of self-pity.

"She's overcome, KJ. She's overcome." I roll my eyes at Shay's dramatic, if accurate, assessment of the situation.

"What's overcome mean?"

"It means your mommy is so happy to be here that instead

of laughing and being happy, her brain got confused and she started to cry. I mean, I almost cried, too. Didn't you?"

The teasing in Shay's voice serves its purpose. KJ laughs.

"No, I didn't cry. I'm a big boy."

"Big boys can cry. In fact, I think I see a tear right there!"

KJ squeals, and I smile into Bati's chest. That girl is a great aunt, man.

"Is she well? We are almost at the transport center."

Ah'dan peeks around from his place in the front of the pod. His light yellow eyes are creased with concern. He looks down to me and then back up at his brother.

"We are fine," Bati returns and pulls me a little closer to him. I don't pull away. It feels too good to pull away.

A few minutes later, the pod, which has been hovering forward at steady intervals, comes to a smooth stop. I feel a light pat on my butt where Bati's hand rests.

"Our visitation agent will have to speak with you," he says gently. I move to lift off of his lap, but he stops me. He lifts me and turns me around, so that I face the side of the pod that is in front of the floating booth. A larger window has opened, and an even-expressioned Lyqa male is seated in the booth on the other side. He says something in their language to Ah'dan.

"If you are able, please speak in English, so our guests can understand you," Ah'dan requests, kindly.

"You are returning from Earth?" the Lyqa repeats without missing a beat. His accent, like Bati's and his family's, is soft and musical.

"We are."

"And how many guests have you returned with?" He's facing the inside of his booth. His hands move over something I can't see.

"There are three in our pod. My mother, father and brother have arrived as well with two more humans. One is the *lehti* to our brother."

"Your brother's *lehti,* she will reside?"

"I believe so."

"And these guests? Will they reside?"

He looks up, finally. His startlingly purple eyes fall on me since I am the closest. Amina wasn't lying about these Lyqa dudes. They are fine. This guy is a little older, maybe close to middle age, but he's still very good looking. His stark white hair is buzzed low, an interesting contrast to his lightly tanned skin. He stares patiently at me as he waits for my answer. I look up to Bati.

"Is he asking us if we're going to live here?"

"Oh, snap, we can stay?"

LaShay's head pops into the isle. Her eyes are wide with excitement.

"Shay…"

"Don't 'Shay' me. If I can stay, I'm staying. Can I stay?" The agent nods and turns back inside the booth.

"You have permission to stay on Lyqa for the equivalent of four Earth months. For permanent residence, you must be *leht* —my implant is not supplying the English translation for this word—"

"It does not matter," Ah'dan cuts in.

"You must be *leht* to a Lyqa partner, the parent to a Lyqa, or complete our citizenship process, which may only be applied for at the end of your four month stay, contingent upon appropriate behavior while visiting."

"Oh," LaShay's face drops comically. "Well, sign me up for the four month pass, then. Is that all right?" She looks to Bati.

"Of course," he returns.

"Yes!" Shay pumps her fist then holds her arm out to the agent when he asks for it. He fits her with a slim bracelet. A small green light blinks on the top of it.

"Will you reside?" The agent turns back to me. Bati shifts

beneath me before replying in Lyqa. The agent nods again and his hands move inside the booth.

"Will the child also reside?"

"Wait, I can stay?" I angle my head up at Bati. He leans down and places a quick kiss on the tip of my nose, surprising me with the easy show of affection.

"You can if you wish, my *lehti*."

"Hey, how come Tee gets to reside and I don't?" Shay whines.

That's a good question. Bati ignores my curious stare and says something else in Lyqa. The agent produces a small bracelet from inside the booth.

"May I see your arm, little one?"

KJ, who's been quietly observing everything from beside Shay, looks at me. I ease out of Bati's lap and crouch down in the isle. I pull him in front of me so that we both face the open panel of the pod.

"It's okay, baby. It's just a cool little bracelet. It doesn't hurt or anything, does it, Shay?"

Shay holds out her arm, twisting it so the fitted bit of metal reflects the dull lights of the pod. "Nope. Not a bit."

Hesitantly, KJ holds his arm out. The agent smiles and closes the band around his wrist. Then he pats my son's hand.

"Ask your *apha* to show you all of the fun things you can do with this." He gestures to Bati. KJ jerks his head up and down quickly and rushes back into his seat.

"And you, ma'am, you can also use this band for any purchases or services you may need. It will code itself to your genetic and residence markers. Your *lehti*'s accounts have already been connected."

"Oh, I don't need any accounts. I'm not going to buy anything here." I think about the two credit cards I have back home, both nearly maxed out. The last thing I need is intergalactic debt.

"You do not have to worry about money here, Tiani. You are free to purchase anything you desire."

"Uh, okay." I agree, just because it's easier. I guess it's better to have it and not need it, than need it and not have it.

The agent smiles and waves us forward. "I hope you enjoy your stay on Lyqa. Welcome."

Ah'dan replies in Lyqa and reaches through the window to grasp the man's arm briefly before tapping the control panel and propelling us forward.

"Tee, dude, we're on an alien planet!"

I look around at Shay and smile. Holy crap, we are.

BATI

Tiani is definitely different. Unlike Amina, she looks at everything. The moment we step outside of the transport center, her head turns in every direction as she takes in her new surroundings.

Her excitement pleases me. KJ, too, curiously walks about the front of the transport center.

"Hi!" he waves at a young Lyqa couple a few feet away. They turn, their surprise at seeing a human child evident.

"Hello, little one," the male says and brushes a hand over KJ's head. The woman, a beautiful raven haired Lyqa with bright hazel eyes, kneels down next to him and pulls him into a gentle hug.

"Where have you come from?" she asks.

"Chicago!" KJ throws his hands up in the air as he bounces with excitement. The woman laughs and looks to me for understanding.

"They are from Earth," I supply. "My *dahni* has never traveled before."

Her face brightens and she smiles at KJ's display of delight.

He bounces away and resumes waving at every passing Lyqa.

"K, stay close to mommy." The anxious voice of my *lehti* sounds out behind me. I turn to find her glowering at me and the woman. A breeze blows from her direction, and I scent… jealousy? It washes over me and my skin trembles.

"I hope your family enjoys their stay here," the woman extends with a knowing smile. She takes hold of my arm briefly before walking back to her pod where her partner is unloading their packs.

"KJ, let us return to your mother." I take the boy's hand and walk back over to Tiani. The smell of jealousy is even more potent.

"Do you know her?"

I tilt my head, confused as to why she is so unsettled. "I do not."

"Oh, she touched you."

I try to contain my urge to smile, but it is difficult. My mouth tilts up with pleasure. I do not mind that she doesn't want other women to touch me.

"Lyqa are an affectionate species. We touch each other often."

"Mm hm." Her mouth twists up to the side before she takes KJ's hand and turns to catch up with the others who are already making their way toward our home.

"It's so quiet."

Tiani's observation is a hushed murmur. Our large party makes its way through the nearly empty streets. She's on my right. KJ is on my other side. His excitement is a vibrant jolt through our joined palms. Ahead, my mother and father lead the group. Tiani's mother walks with them, her arm linked somewhat stiffly through my father's arm. Kwarq and Amina walk with Ah'dan in front of us. Amina's round form moves slowly, keeping the general pace easy.

The thick vegetation lining the homes beside us rustles gently in the breeze. The sounds of insect life reach my ears, but aside from that, it is, in fact, very quiet.

"I have not noticed until now, but you are correct. Lyqa senses are very sensitive. As such, we have designed our homes to contain most sound. Otherwise, it would be overwhelming."

"Wow," Tiani looks up at a large clay structure beside us. Dim lights glow behind the window coverings. The shadows of Lyqa move against them. "So, all of these houses are soundproof?"

"They are."

"Even on the inside? What if you need to call someone in the house?"

I smile. "The insides of our homes are open. It is easier for us to ignore select sounds. We can usually grant privacy when it is necessary."

"Hm. So if someone is doing it, you can choose to listen or not?"

"KJ, come here. I have something to show you." Ah'dan's voice calls back to us. KJ breaks free of my hand and runs ahead, launching himself at my brother who lifts him over his head and settles him on his shoulders. I'm left alone with my *lehti*.

"I assume you refer to sex," I reply. "Yes, if someone in our home requires privacy with their partner, it is considerate to focus one's attention elsewhere."

"What if they're loud? Like really, really loud?"

My mouth twitches. "Some partners make it more difficult than others. Your sister, for instance, made it quite hard." She makes an uncomfortable face, and I cannot stop my grin. "You also presented a particular challenge to my family during your sister's wedding."

Chapter 8

TIANI

"Like this?"

KJ waves his hand over the sensor, prompting the door to the bedroom to swish open.

"Just like that, my *dahni*. This is your room now. You can come and go as you please, as long as you let your mother know."

Bati guides KJ through the door, and I step in behind them. The room is large. Much too large for one four-year-old. In the corner, there's a bed a little smaller than a twin-size on Earth. The rest of the room is an open space. All across the room are toys and other things a kid would go crazy over. What looks like a mini jungle gym sits in the middle of the room. KJ jets into the room and makes a beeline for it, pausing with a hand on one of the lower rungs. Bati laughs and makes a shooing motion with his hands.

"Go ahead, my *dahni*, everything in this room is yours."

With an excited giggle, KJ propels himself up on the first rung. He pulls himself up hand over foot with little grunts of effort until he gets to the padded top. He jumps to his feet, raising his fists above his head triumphantly. Bati whoops and claps his hands together.

"You are quick, KJ. Well done. Now can you get down?"

KJ creeps to the edge and peers over. His mouth pulls down. I chuckle and shake my head. I knew the moment he started climbing that getting back down would be less enthusiastic. I move to go help him, but Bati beats me, his long legs eating up the space before I've taken a step. He's so tall that he merely plucks KJ from the top and sets him on the ground. He ruffles his hand over my son's head.

"I am going to show your mother to her room. Will you be okay playing here until we get back?"

KJ runs over to a pile of metal blocks. They look heavy, but KJ picks two of the rectangles up easily and stacks them together. He jumps back when the pieces shift and forge together into one piece.

"These are special blocks, KJ. You can make any shape you wish." Bati squats down next to him and points to a square. "Wave your hand over it."

KJ shakes his left hand over the chunk of metal and a crystal clear projection rises from its surface. On the display are several shapes.

"Choose this one." Bati points to the image of a cylinder that rotates in the projection.

"How?" KJ's head is close to the little screen. He's unsure of how to interact with it.

"Just use your finger and touch the one you want."

KJ lifts his hand and jabs at the image of the cylinder before jerking his hand and body back. My eyes widen with his when the block lifts and shifts, the metal rearranging itself, the edges smoothing and constricting, until a cylinder sits in its place.

"Cool!"

Bati chuckles again and lifts the newly formed block, handing it over to my son.

"Make something very cool for me to see," he says, using the new word. "I will be back in a moment."

KJ starts to wave his hand over all of the blocks, turning each one into a new shape. He cackles loudly when a block shifts and twists until it sits in a star shape. Bati rises and walks back to me where I'm still standing at the door.

"Thank you for letting him use all this stuff. Those blocks are pretty cool. They're like little transformers."

"I do not know what those are, but these are common toys for Lyqa children. They are safe, and these are his to enjoy. I will show you to your room now." He moves past me, and his arm brushes against my body, sending a little shiver of awareness through me.

"K, don't get back on that thing until we come back, okay." I point to the jungle gym. KJ jerks his head up and down without looking up from one of the shifting blocks. I don't think he's going to get much building done.

I follow Bati back into the large living room area of his part of the house. He lives in a mansion, or at least that's what it would be on Earth. But really, it's just a large main house with connected smaller residences. Kwarq and Amina disappeared to one of these smaller "apartments" when he first arrived. Bati led us to another. I have no idea how many apartments are connected, but it looked like everyone headed in a different direction.

When we enter, Shay rushes in from the open balcony doors and ducks around Bati, grabbing hold of his shirt and hiding her face against his back. I get the strange urge to push her away.

"Ohmygod! Get rid of it. It's gonna get me!"

A loud buzz draws my eyes back to the open doors where a huge, bright red bug is hovering at the entrance. Its large neon blue wings look like spider webs fluttering beside its scaly body. It darts forward, the buzz getting louder, and I automatically grab hold of Bati's arm, using the other half of his torso to shield myself as much as I can.

"What the hell is that?"

Bati's shoulders flinch up and down. "It is just a bug."

"It's just a bug? That thing is fucking huge! Can it bite us?"

Again, that shrug. "It can, of course. This type of beetle has a viciously sharp stinger, but it will not harm you unless it is threatened."

The buzzing sounds closer, so I peek around Bati's shoulder. The bug hovers right in front of him. I yelp and duck back behind him.

"Dude, get rid of it!" Me and Shay both yell out at the same time.

Bati turns, shifting the shield of his body. We move with him, ducking low just in case.

"I cannot make it leave, *lehti*, but I promise if you calm down, it will not harm you." He stops moving and sighs deeply when we grip him tighter and refuse to move from behind him.

"Just kill it!" Shay screams out when it flies high and swoops around us.

"We do not kill things if we do not have to here." There is real admonishment in his tone. "Now, please, it has left. If you will let me close the balcony doors, I can prevent it from coming back in."

He starts walking toward the patio, and we both have no choice but to let go of him. The moment he steps away, we grab each other, both of us looking around cautiously.

Bati closes the doors and turns back to us. He crosses his arms and raises an eyebrow at us cowering together.

"You both look ridiculous."

We do. I realize it the moment he says so, and I step away from LaShay, smoothing my shirt down as I try to play it off.

"Earth bugs are a lot smaller," I mumble with as much

pride as I can.

"And yet you kill them? Why kill something that is of no harm to you?"

Me and Shay exchange a look. We really don't have an answer. Bati waits for a moment, and when we don't respond, he shakes his head and walks past us, waving for us to follow him.

He leads us to another room, just off the living room, waving his hand over the side of the door and causing it to slide back on itself.

"We normally do not close doors in our home, but if you need privacy, just wave your hand over the entrance."

I'm surprised that the room is about a third of the size of the one he gave KJ. A large bed takes up most of the space. A few intricately designed vases are arranged in the corners. A wide angled table takes up one side of the room, and a long, cushy lounge sits against the wall opposite the bed.

It doesn't look like a guest room. It looks lived in. It also has the distinct scent of wood and spice. It's a scent I have smelled before, and my body reacts to it, getting warm in all the right places. My heart trips a little and I turn to Bati.

"Is this your room?"

"It is, but I will reside in the common room for now."

I start to shake my head, but Shay walks past us and throws herself onto the bed. Again, there is that urge to drag her off of the place where he sleeps. I stamp it down and turn back to Bati.

"You don't have to do that for us. We can sleep out there. We're small. You'll probably be uncomfortable." The low couch in the living room is short and hard looking. Whereas Bati's bed is clearly sized for Lyqa height.

"It is no problem, Tiani. You must accept and allow me to be a proper host."

I look over to the bed where LaShay is lying face down.

Her eyes are closed. At first, I think she's faking, but then a loud snore sounds out in the room.

"It is late, well past the evening hour. You must be tired. I will let you prepare to sleep." He gives one of those short head nods and leaves, waving the door closed after him.

I can't sleep, and I have to pee. I never sleep well in new places. Unlike Shay, who could fall asleep standing up in the middle of her high school graduation—a real thing that happened—I take forever to get comfortable. It doesn't help that every time I try to get situated, a big puff of Bati whiffs around me. Damn that Lyqa dude smells good.

After he left earlier, I unpacked my and LaShay's suitcases and went to go put KJ to bed, only to find him dressed in some kind of jersey type shirt and shorts set, already asleep in the little bed. Everything in the room had been put away, and his clothes and other items had been removed from his bag and placed into the single dresser in the room.

When I passed the living room on my way back to Bati's room, he was arranging a bunch of large cushions on the floor, stacking them until they made a somewhat comfortable looking bed. He looked up and smiled.

"Thank you for seeing to KJ. That was sweet, but I don't want you to feel like you have to take care of him."

"It is my pleasure to care for him. He is a very wonderful child. It is no trouble. Sleep well, Tiani."

"You also don't have to sleep out here, we really don't mind."

"It is okay. Your sister is already asleep. I would not wake her."

"You can always slide into bed with her, and I can sleep out here. She might kick you in the face, though."

He'd actually looked pissed.

"I would not lay with another. Not even to sleep."

"I was kidding," I'd returned and gone for a joking laugh, but he'd just frowned harder.

"Not even in jest."

We'd stood there, staring at each other. Me wanting to do nothing more than leap over that couch and tackle him to the ground. Eventually, I'd said goodnight and went back to the room.

Now I'm up staring at the wall. And I've gotta pee.

"Ugh!" I fling off the thin, super-soft sheet. A fresh cloud of Bati floats around me, and I have to close my eyes against the shiver that skates through my body.

I slip off the bed and tiptoe over to the door. When I wave my hand at the point where the door meets the wall, it slides open with a soft whoosh.

It's dark. Like pitch black. A sliver of light peeks in from the curtains over the balcony, but other than that, I can barely see my hand in front of my face.

I move into the hall, trying to remember what everything looked like, so I don't run into anything. I walk a few feet and pause considering where to go, before I realize Bati never told us where the bathroom was.

"Shit."

The soft curse echoes in the silence of the apartment, and I can almost hear KJ saying, "Ooo, Mommy you cursed," in my head.

Just around the corner, I can hear the faint sound of humming. It reaches me in the quiet, and I send a thank you up to the universe that Bati is still awake. I tiptoe in that direction. Luckily, the couches and pillows are white, so I'm able to make them out in the darkness. As I round the couch, the outline of Bati's large, dark body comes into view, and I suck in the breath.

Even in silhouette, he's fine. He's lying on his back with his head turned to the side. That sound I heard was not him humming at all. It's the sound of him snoring. The soft musical noise floats up from the floor, and I'm drawn closer to it, crouching down until I'm kneeling at his head. My hand reaches out on its own to touch the sharp plane of his cheekbone.

His skin is smooth and cool to the touch. My fingertips slide down his cheek. A hint of hair, as soft as a baby's, feathers across my fingers. Kwarq has a beard. Bati would also look good with facial hair, but I'm glad he stays clean shaven. It lets me see every bit of his face. Every smooth ridge. Every bit of dark, beautiful skin.

"Are you unable to sleep, Tiani?"

The bright blue of Bati's eyes is like a glittering jewel in the dark. I jerk my hand back, but Bati moves Lyqa quick, catching it. His hold is gentle. He glides down my arm until he has my hand clasped firmly and pulls me forward. His head turns just before I feel the press of his full lips into my palm.

"I—uh—I have to use the bathroom. I, I have to pee. You never told us where the bathroom was."

"This is why you are touching me while I sleep?"

"What? No. You were humming."

"I was not."

"No, I mean, I thought you were humming, but you were snoring. It sounded like humming."

"I do not snore." Even in the dark, I can see his look of disbelief.

"You do. It sounds like music."

"I was thinking of you as I slept."

"Dreaming." The word is barely a sound between us.

"I do not know this word."

"That's what it's called when you think of someone while you're sleeping. It's called dreaming."

I'm yanked forward when he pulls suddenly on my hand. I

catch myself with my free hand, but still I'm only an inch away from his face when I stop.

"I was dreaming of you," he whispers between our mouths, and when I inhale, the breath is minty.

My eyes have adjusted. His skin seems to reflect the dark. It bounces off the blue, making him look like he's made of opal. A black diamond laid out beneath me.

"I want you, Bati." I do. I can barely breathe I want him so badly. I lower my face, wanting to be closer. Wanting to feel that creepy tongue of his. I'm almost there. His breath fans up into my face in minty waves. Just when our lips are about to touch, he turns his head away. My mouth makes contact with his ear, and I pull back.

"The room to relieve yourself is down that hall to the left, Tiani." His voice is strangled and tense.

"Right. Thanks." He lets my arm go, and I push back to my feet, standing back over him.

"Sleep well, my *lehti*." He turns to his side, putting his back to me.

"Goodnight."

I find the bathroom easy enough. Although, it takes me some time to figure out how the lights work. In the end, I wave my hands around enough and eventually, they brighten enough for me to see myself to the toilet.

When I pass through the living room on my way back to bed, that soft hum floats over me again, and every step away from the sound makes it more clear to me how stupid I've been.

BATI

"Does your back hurt, brother?"

I redirect the piece of fruit I'm about to put into my mouth and toss it at Ah'dan's head. He stretches his neck, catching it cleanly between his teeth, and laughs.

"You're terrible at throwing. You've always been terrible at throwing."

"Stop talking, brother." I consider throwing another piece of fruit, but he's right, I've never had good aim. Continuing to try and hit him would only end in me feeding him my breakfast.

"So, you're just going to sleep on the floor forever."

"Not forever."

"Then until when?" He picks through the basket of fruit on the counter until he finds another *kisi*.

"She doesn't love me," My first heart aches at the admission.

"I heard her come to you."

I jerk my head around to glare at my brother. "You were listening?"

He sighs and rolls his eyes, an annoying habit he learned from Amina.

"I wasn't listening. I heard. There is a difference."

"You don't have to hear."

He shrugs and takes a large bite of his fruit, spraying a fine mist of juice across the table.

"Why did you reject her?"

"I didn't reject her. I gave her directions to the restroom." I take a bite of my *kisi*. The sweet, tangy flesh reminds me of the taste of Tiani's mouth when I kissed her last. The taste of the Earth fruit called orange. It was the hardest thing I've ever done to not kiss her last night, even though things have been different. She has been…lighter, but that doesn't mean she is ready to accept the *leht*.

Ah'dan rolls his eyes again.

"I could smell her rejection from across the house. I could smell all of her from across the house. And I'm sure just then she wanted more than directions to the restroom."

I can't stop my hand from hurling the leftover *kisi,* and I'm glad when it glances off the side of Ah'dan's shoulder. He looks down at his shirt and the bright pink stain from the juice and shakes his head, trouncing my bit of triumph. He's less than five feet away. My aim is pathetic.

"Bati!"

Luckily, my ability to catch is better than my ability to throw, and I turn just in time to intercept KJ's launch through the air. He laughs as I grab hold of him and swing him up on the counter.

"These are cool. I jumped *all the way up there*!" he stretches his tiny hand up as far as it will go. I look down at his feet. Strapped to each is a round-bottomed shoe made from the springy sponges of Qiton's west swamps. The thick soles allow the wearer to jump to great heights. I'm not sure how these got mixed in with the toys we selected for KJ, but one look at the smirk on Ah'dan's face gives me a clue. I shoot him a scowl, and he snorts.

"I do not think these are safe for you to play with, my *dahni*. Maybe when you are a little older." I pull the shoes off of KJ's feet and place them on the counter. The little boy's chest huffs a big puff of air and he crosses his arms over his chest.

"I knew you were going to say that," he pouts, and I bite back my smile.

"You did?"

He gives a sulky nod.

"Then why did you put them on?"

"I wanted to have fun."

Ah'dan snickers quietly behind me, and I have to stop myself from joining him. I will have to watch my brother. He has always been an encourager of trouble.

"How about we find a safe way to have fun? A way that will not have your mother angry with me, yes?"

"Okay."

He drops his arms. A bright pink drop of *kisi* juice is on the counter next to him. He pokes his finger into the glob and brings it to his outstretched tongue. Immediately, his face scrunches up. His mouth twists and his eyes squeeze shut.

"Bleh!" He sputters and flicks his tongue in and out, trying to rid it of the taste.

This time I do laugh. "It does not taste good?"

I laugh louder when KJ pulls the hem of his shirt up to rub it against his tongue. *Kisi* is one of my favorite fruits. The meat is sweet and slightly tangy. I could eat a dozen and never tire of them.

"It's yucky." He smacks his lips together again. "Too sour."

"Try this." Ah'dan holds out a sliver of *bom*. The bright yellow meat is crunchy when raw, but bland. It is used often in salads to balance stronger flavors.

KJ is hesitant as he reaches out for it. He brings it to his mouth and takes the tiniest bite. Both Ah'dan and I wait for his reaction. He chews once before his mouth opens, letting the *bom* fall back out.

"That," he points at the ribbed stalk Ah'dan holds in his hand, "tastes like kaka."

I don't know what kaka is, but I can tell by KJ's face that it is not something with an appealing flavor.

Ten minutes later, we've cut into a half dozen different fruits, but we finally find something that doesn't result in a comical reaction of disgust.

"It tastes like banana," KJ mumbles around a mouthful of *sawa*.

"Is banana a good fruit? Do most people like banana?"

"Bananas are good. Mommy has a banana for breakfast every day." His little legs kick against the base of the counter.

Sawa is the least interesting of the fruits we have offered him. The flesh is juicy and not very sweet, but KJ munches happily, biting off another chunk of the round, fuzzy, purple fruit to add to what's already in his mouth.

"Slow down, my *dahni*, you will choke."

He chews slowly and swallows before taking another bite. I leave him to his breakfast and go to gather all of the remaining *sawa* to set it aside for Tiani and her mother and sisters.

"Can we do something fun?"

I turn back to KJ. He's finished the *sawa*. The large inner seed lays discarded on the table. I lift him from the counter and place him on his feet. Taking his hand, I place the seed in his palm.

"Let me show you how to dispose of your trash."

I walk him over to the disposal and instruct him to wave his hand over the sensor. When it opens, he tosses the seed inside.

"Where did it go?" He angles his head to peer into the dark shoot.

"It is collected and redistributed to a farm, so it can grow again."

"Oh."

I leave him peering into the disposal and go back to the counter to help Ah'dan clear the remainder of the fruits we cut for KJ's tasting. They may not be to human liking, but my family will eat them.

"Can we go to the park?"

I look down to where KJ peers up at me. He has told me he is four-years-old, but he is so small. So much smaller than a Lyqa child, although no less bright. Perhaps even more so.

"What is the park?" I ask. My language implant is showing me an open, grassy area, but that could be anywhere on Lyqa. Does he wish to be outside?

"You know, a park. With swings and slides and stuff to play on."

I do not know.

"I do not think we have parks here, but I can take you out if you would like to run and play."

"Qiton has something like what he describes," Ah'dan offers from the other side of the counter where he's munching on the leftover fruit. He's right. I remember the large open recreation grounds where Qitoni children gathered to play and climb and generally behave freely. It is where the tower in KJ's room was made.

"Can we go to Kee-tone?" KJ asks, his pronunciation making me smile.

"If you like, but we will have to ask your mother."

"You know, KJ, you should ask your *apha* to take you on *ta'ani maul*. It is very fun."

KJ's face lights up. "Oh, yeah, I want to go to tommy-mall!" he shouts excitedly, bouncing up and down on his toes.

I chuckle and run my hand over his head. "I do not think you are old enough for *ta'ani maul*, my *dahni*."

Ah'dan scoffs.

"You completed your first *ta'ani* when about his age. It would be fun for him, and a good chance for you to spend time as father and son." He says, switching to Lyqa.

"I don't think his mother would appreciate me whisking her son off to another planet when she has just arrived on this one," I return in our language.

"Then take her with you," he responds casually, and I want to knock him upside the head.

"That will not work."

"Why? She has been different since we came here. Maybe Earth was too stressful for her. She has nothing to fear now. Maybe that freedom will allow her to love you."

KJ's head swivels back and forth between me and my brother the way a child's does when he's waiting for adults to decide.

"Can we go?" his impatience is getting the best of him. He's bouncing again.

"Can you go where?"

Everyone turns at the sound of Tiani's voice as she walks into the kitchen. She's wearing one of my shirts. I didn't notice last night, even though my eyesight is superb in the dark. But I notice now, and the sight of her toned, brown legs moving beneath my top makes me flinch in my loose pants.

"Bati is going to take me to tommy-mall!" KJ announces and bounces over to his mother. She lifts him beneath the arms and settles him on her hip, causing the shirt to ride up on one side. I lift my eyes from the smooth curve of her thigh. Help me.

"You guys have malls here?"

"Malls?" My voice is tense. I clear my throat.

"Yeah, places where there are a bunch of stores in one place to shop."

"Ah, we have a market for this purpose. You can purchase food, clothing, goods. Do you have need to visit the market?"

She shrugs. I notice she isn't really meeting my eyes.

"Not really, but it might be cool to go. Just to check it out. I mean, is it safe? Are people going to trip cause we're human?"

I shake my head. "Lyqa are kind people. We do not hurt others merely for being different. It would be safe for us to go."

KJ claps his hands and bounces against his mother's hip. "Yay, we're going to tommy-mall!"

Tiani laughs. "Why is he calling it that?"

"He is saying *ta'ani maul*. It is a kind of activity. I was suggesting to my brother that he should take you and your son. It would be fun."

I cut my eyes over to Ah'dan, who ignores me. I know

what he is trying to do, but forcing me alone with Tiani and her son will not make her love me.

"It is not something for children," I return, and face Tiani again. She's looking at me now, and the jolt of awareness when I lock onto her dark eyes takes my breath away.

"What kind of activity is it?"

"It is a kind of outing. Like a scavenger hunt. You go to another location and complete some simple tasks, enjoy the outdoors, experience the culture of another place," Ah'dan supplies.

"It's dangerous?"

"Not at all, my *sa'aih*. It is harmless fun. Children do it all the time. We completed them with our father when we were about KJ's age."

I shoot Ah'dan another look. "We completed them when we were his age, but we are Lyqa. He is not."

"So, you're saying my kid can't do it because he's human?"

I turn back to Tiani, and her eyes are narrowed on me. "No, my *lehti,* I am not implying he cannot do it—I—"

"Then why don't you want to take us?"

"You would come as well?" The idea is almost too tempting to think about. I hold my breath, hoping I haven't misunderstood.

"I mean, I don't have to. I trust you to keep him safe. I just thought you meant all of us."

"You have not misunderstood," I hurry to correct her. "I would like to take you. For us to go. All of us."

She smiles and it's sweet and shy. "So, you'll take us?"

My breath catches in my throat. She is so beautiful, my *lehti,* that I could never tell her no.

"I will take you, but we will have to visit the market to gather supplies and get you both proper clothing. The people of Qiton have a very unique fashion. It helps to blend in."

* * *

"Does it have to have so much material?" Tiani's eyebrows raise skeptically as the modiste wraps another layer of sheer fabric around her middle. She pins it at Tiani's shoulder and turns her around to begin her skirt.

"It is the fashion on Qiton. They prefer their layers," I say from my seat behind her. Right now, I am glad for the plethora of fabric. It is the only way I have managed to make my cock relax.

When we first entered the shop, the modiste had wasted no time stripping off Tiani's clothes after I told her what kind of dress to make. I'd attempted to excuse myself to wait in another room, but Tiani stopped me.

"It's not like you haven't seen me before," she'd said and waved me into the seat. "Besides, you know what this is supposed to look like. You have to make sure she makes me look good." And she'd winked. It was a surprisingly playful gesture. In fact, everything about Tiani has been less tense and more playful since we came to Lyqa.

"Anything you wear would be beautiful, Tiani."

I'd meant it. The only thing she looks better in is nothing at all. The moment her firm, high breasts had been bared, I'd focused on the far wall of the shop. Now I am grateful for every bit of cloth the modiste places over her, even as my heart aches as she is covered from me.

After an hour of sitting rigidly in my seat, Tiani's dress is finally complete. The modiste helps Tiani back into her Earth clothes as I pretend to examine a display of jewelry. Despite my indifferent inspection of the jewels, something catches my eye. It's a ring. A large, square diamond, as blue as any ocean on Qiton and as clear as any glass blown on Pahashi, and set in the finest metal from the Lyqa mountains. I think of the human custom of proposal. When Kwarq proposed to Amina, she'd cried. Even Tiani's eyes had glistened briefly. Her heart had fluttered with longing. I feel that same longing now.

"Ready?"

I tear my eyes from the beautiful ring, and I clear my throat, which is suddenly tight with emotion. When I turn to face her, I've managed to hide most of my feelings.

"I am."

TIANI

Bati taps his wrist band and a crystal clear projection of Ah'dan springs up in front of him. Kinda like Lyqa Facetime, except way cooler.

"Tiani and I are going to stroll through the market. Meet us with KJ at the fountain in an hour?" he follows this with a string of Lyqa. Ah'dan's projection shows him clearly rolling his eyes before the projection cuts off.

"Come, let us take our time. I would show you my city."

Bati holds out his hand. I hesitate before taking it. His gentle grip swallows my hand, and a charge of sexual tension bolts through me. I was really salty about him rejecting my kiss last night, but it all floats away when our palms meet. I find myself smiling as we walk through the crowded market.

"Just so it does not alarm you, my people may stare. Most Lyqa have never seen a human. However, you are in no danger."

People are staring. They mostly look curious. Some smile and nod their heads or wave. A young girl, she looks about ten human years old, flaps her hand frantically at me as we pass. I wave back, and she bursts into a fit of giggles.

"Lehti yah'san!" Her wispy, lyrical voice floats over me.

"Nah'ah lehti qaa yah'san," Bati returns. He looks down at me, and his expression is tender.

The girl skips back to her parents who wait patiently a few feet away. I lean in to Bati's side. "What did she say?"

"She said you are beautiful."

"Really?" I look back to the girl, who's still watching me. I smile and give a little head nod in appreciation. She grins widely back.

"And what did you say?"

"I said you were the most beautiful."

A warm flush rushes over me. I don't think I've ever pseudo-blushed so much in my life since I've met Bati. He makes me feel like I'm the shit for real.

"Thank you," I say when I get myself under control.

"Of course, Tiani. Let us try some Lyqa foods."

He leads me away, seemingly unaware of how much he's just stroked my ego. We pass a stall stacked with what looks like pies. A male Lyqa stands behind the table. When I see him, I can't stop the quick patter of my heart. I press a hand to my chest to stop it. It's beating so hard, I'm worried Bati will hear.

"Would you like a taste?"

Would I? I stamp the thought down, but I'd be a lie if I said I didn't think the guy in front of me isn't shamefully good-looking.

Like all Lyqa, he's kind of strange to look at. His skin is light reddish brown. Thick, jet black hair hangs down either side of his head and disappears down his back. Narrow, single-lidded green eyes peer warmly at me. My gaze fixes on the flex of his biceps as he reaches out a hand holding a small, flaky triangle.

"It is a fruit pie. Try it."

I look up at Bati. His mouth is curved in an amused smirk.

I want to, but I can't take it without touching him and I'm honestly scared to. My reaction to him, even if it isn't exactly sexual, is still a bit embarrassing.

"He will not bite you, Tiani. I promise. Even though it smells as if you would like him to."

My eyes widen. I open my mouth to deny it, but Bati leans

down and gives me a knowing look. His mouth is an inch from mine. It curves at one corner, making him appear boyish and cute.

"Do you think he cannot smell your attraction?"

"That's not what it is. I'm not attracted to him," I mumble, even though I know everybody within a hundred yards can hear me.

"Hm. Well, you must try the pie now. If only to soothe my kinsman's feelings."

My eyes jump to the guy, expecting to see offense on his face, but he's grinning.

"Your *lehti* is teasing you. Please do not believe me to be offended, but I must also insist that you taste the pie."

The English words are spoken carefully. His deep voice kind of sings over me, and that rush of nervousness skitters through my middle. I reach out and take the triangle with a slightly shaking hand, flinching when my fingers brush over his palm. He watches me with that same patient smile.

They wait as I bring the pie to my mouth and take a bite. I work hard on schooling my features as my teeth pierce the crispy crust. I have no idea what I'm in for.

Oh my god, it's...gross. I force myself to chew; although, everything in me is saying spit this shit out. The filling is sour and a strange slimy texture. It tastes like sweetened okra mixed with lemon. It's terrible. I close my eyes and try to chew faster. I just have to get it down my throat. My jaw starts to cramp as I work to get the mouthful soft enough to swallow. Beside me, Bati chuckles.

"You may spit it out if you like, Tiani."

I open my eyes. I have no idea what my face looks like, but it feels like I've got major stank face going on despite my best efforts.

The guy is holding a napkin out to me. I grab it and hold it over my mouth, quickly spitting the half-chewed pie into the middle.

"I'm so sorry. Oh my god, I would never do that, normally. It isn't bad. It's just too sour. I'm so sorry."

"It is no offense, *sa'qi*. *Kisi* is an acquired taste."

"Oh, god. I'm so sorry." I keep apologizing. Mostly because I'm literally scraping my tongue with the napkin. The sourness lingers on my palate, making my jaw ache. I feel like such a jerk, but I tried. I really did.

"You are human?" The guy looks at me closely. That nervousness returns.

"Yes," I respond and mentally shake my head when my voice isn't as strong as I want it to be. What is wrong with me?

"I have never met a human before. You are quite a beautiful people. My name is S'wad. It is nice to meet you."

"Uh, I'm Tee. Tiani. Thanks. I mean, it's good to meet you, too." God, I'm acting like I've never introduced myself to anyone before.

"Hm. Well, Tiani. Hopefully, next time, I will have something more to your liking."

I nod my thanks and let Bati steer me away. My face burns as we walk from the stall.

"That wasn't mortifying at all," I mumble sarcastically.

"You are embarrassed?"

I turn a surprised expression on him. "Seriously? I practically drooled all over that poor guy. I don't know what the hell that was."

Bati chuckles. "It was nature. He is an attractive male. It would be disingenuous to pretend not to notice."

"Yeah, but, you know. You were there. It was weird. I didn't want him or anything."

"I know."

"You do?"

Bati smiles and taps his nose. "I can smell you, Tiani. You

may have found him attractive, but I did not sense desire."

"Oh, okay." I still feel silly, even though Bati doesn't seem bothered. Maybe jealousy isn't a Lyqa thing. Bati shakes his head and pulls me against his side. The contact washes away the nerves from my interaction with the baker and replaces it with a blitz of heat. He inhales. A low pleasant hum purrs from his chest.

"This, Tiani, what you are feeling right now, is desire."

It takes us another half hour to reach the place where we're supposed to meet Ah'dan. The moment we turn the corner into the market square, I spot my son. When I see Ah'dan, I gasp. Beside me, Bati snorts and it sounds like he's trying to smother a laugh.

"KJ!" My voice is a harsh rebuke. This kid!

KJ pushes off from the fountain where he and Ah'dan wait and skips over to us with a happy smile on his face. His mouth is covered in something blue and sticky, and he raises similarly colored palms up next to his shoulders, his eyes wide with innocence.

"What? Uncle Ah'dan said I could have them."

Ah'dan's eyes cut down to my son. It's clear from his expression exactly how much of a hand he had in the accumulation of packages he's struggling to hold in his arms. It's obvious from the shape of many of the packages that they're mostly toys.

I narrow my eyes.

"Uncle Ah'dan, huh?" He nods enthusiastically, and I fold my lips to stop from smiling. "Well, just because someone says they'll buy you something doesn't mean you should let them. You know better, K."

I knew I should have had the "don't ask for anything" talk before I sent him off with Ah'dan.

"Sorry about that," I tell Ah'dan. "You guys are too nice.

You should have told him no. I'll pay you back for whatever you got him."

Ah'dan's jaw sets firmly. When I glance at Bati, he has the same annoyed expression. "You will not repay me for anything, my *sa'aih*. You are not guests. We are family, and he is my *dah'san*. I reserve the right to spoil him a little from time to time."

"A little? You have like twenty bags!"

"*Tak-siq*, that's twenty-seven in Lyqa. Uncle Ah'dan taught me," KJ pipes up with a self-satisfied grin.

My face shifts to shock, but I manage a tight smile for my son.

"Wow, baby. That's so good!" I force out before looking back to Ah'dan. "Twenty-seven?" I mouth, and he shrugs like he couldn't care less.

"It is good for him to learn about the culture of Lyqa. I did not just buy him toys. I also bought him books and learning aids."

"And candy!" KJ shouts up, his sticky, blue hands waving. Ah'dan rolls his eyes and shifts the packages in his arms, bumping KJ in the back of the head with a softer one. KJ shoots Ah'dan a look and rubs at his head, smearing blue through his hair.

Ah'dan's eyes widen in a silent message for KJ to put a lid on it. My kid doesn't get it. He has no shame. He reaches into his pocket and pulls out a rectangle of what looks like taffy. He pops it in his mouth and looks up at Ah'dan, giving him a big blue grin in response.

Chapter 9

TIANI

"You know, I would give you shit about leaving two days before I'm supposed to give birth, but I can't even pretend to be mad about this." Amina rubs over her big belly. Her stomach hangs low on her body. She moves her hands to her back and arches to counter the weight.

"We can wait until after," I tell her, but she's already shaking her head.

"Uh, no. I want you to go now. Bati said you'll be back right after, and apparently, only me and Kwarq are going to be there when I give birth, so. Plus, I spent my entire time here in the damn house sleeping. You guys should at least see some other stuff."

Bati walks out of the house with a large, square cloth pack slung over his shoulder. He holds a smaller pack in his free hand. Right behind him is KJ. His little legs move awkwardly in the knee length tunic Bati bought for him at the clothing shop. He steps forward to take the first tall step, and I'm about to rush forward to tell him to be careful, but Bati turns around and stops him with a gentle but firm look.

"K, remember how I showed you?"

KJ drops to his butt. He scoots forward and eases down to the next step. He takes the rest of the steps like this, holding tight to the little pack on his back. When he gets to the bottom, he brushes off the back of his tunic and marches to the waiting transport.

"Oh my god! That was so adorable!" Amina squeals, grabbing hold of my arm excitedly.

I watch KJ "help," trying his best to hoist the large pack into the transport. Bati takes hold of the top straps, carrying most of the weight as KJ pushes from the bottom.

When everything is stored, Bati hoists KJ up into his arms. KJ holds his hand up and after a moment of instruction, Bati slaps his palm against my son's smaller one.

"High five!" KJ shouts. Bati's head falls back as a deep, chuckle erupts from his chest. My heart gives a slight skip. It makes me press my hand to my chest in surprise.

"High five," he repeats.

"You're funny, Bati," KJ giggles, hugging him around the neck.

"They're good together," Amina whispers conspiratorially.

"They are," I admit because I can't even deny it. Bati is everything I would want for a father to my son. He is everything Kamar never wanted to be. My heart beats a little quicker, and I thump my fist between my breasts.

"Heart acting funny?"

I follow Amina's eyes down to where my fist is pressed to my chest. "It's beating fast. I think I'm just nervous."

"Mm, hm," she murmurs, her mouth tilting into a little smile.

"Are you ready to depart?"

Bati stands by the transport holding the door open for me. KJ is already inside. His face is pressed to the glass. A little 'o' of fog blooms from his open mouth. I shake my head. This kid.

"I guess. Are you sure I don't need to bring anything else?" Bati insisted that I let him pack. He wouldn't even let me bring a toothbrush.

"I have packed all that we require." He holds his hand out to me. I look back at Amina, but immediately roll my eyes at mile-wide grin on her face. I can't stand her.

When I take his hand, it's warm. His long fingers close over mine, swallowing my hand and sending a tingle up my arm. I settle into the transport and Bati walks around to enter the other side, taking the seat closest to the control panel. He engages, hovering us slowly over the staggered tops of the Lyqa houses.

"We're gonna have fun!" KJ leans forward in his seat, his chest stretched as much as it can against his safety strap.

"We are, my *dahni,*" Bati replies and leans back to brush his hand over KJ's head before turning to me. "Are you ready, Tiani?"

I nod. "Let's do this."

"She is human?"

"She is," Bati replies. They aren't speaking English or even Lyqa. Before we left, Kwarq walked up and stuck something behind my ear. He said it would help me understand the language on Qiton. Still, it's weird to hear the strange moaning sounds the thing makes suddenly become clear words in my head.

The being in front of me looks like something from a nightmare. Lyqas, with their strange features and hulking frames, kind of just look like tall humans. But the guy asking Bati questions as we wait to be allowed entry to Qiton gives me the first real feeling of *alien*.

His skin is a translucent, milky lavender color. I can see right through to the wiry ropes of tendon that criss cross beneath. The skin covering his face is tight. So tight, that at the eyes and mouth, it looks like it's about flip inside out.

Slivers of white membrane line the corners of eyeballs capped in silver. No iris, no pupil, no whites of the eyes. Just swirling silver. When he speaks, the lips stretch wide to let out the wailing sound of his language. With the yards and yards of fabric wrapped around his body and dragging along the floor, he reminds me of a ghost.

"Your hearts are unified," he returns, looking between me and Bati. I'm not sure what he means, but Bati nods, so I assume it's something lost in translation. "You are partnered?" he asks. The Qitoni holds a slim, transparent tablet between boney fingered hands. A long silver nail taps against the screen.

"She is my *lehti,*" Bati replies evenly.

The Qitoni looks to my son and warbles. KJ, who the moment we landed insisted on being carried, jumps and presses his face further into my shoulder. This is a little weird, even for him. His arms are clasped behind my neck tight enough to choke me a little. I rub his back and focus on comforting him, if only to calm my own nerves. This shit is kind of scary.

"This is your young?"

"He is ours."

My eyes jump to Bati's face. The Qitoni catches my look of surprise. The silver cap of his eyes swirl into focus on me, lingering over KJ, before shifting back to Bati. He warbles again. It sounds like gargling.

"He is of you?" the translator supplies in my head. The voice raises slightly at the end. It doesn't sound like he believes it.

Bati pauses, staring calmly at the guy, and I take a moment to glance around. Several Lyqa walk mixed in with the Qitoni. I can tell what they are because they're all tall and beautiful and that strange mix of human features that look both familiar and also so very unsettling. A few feet away are some other species. Their strange forms make me look away quickly. I agreed to come here, but now that I'm thinking about it, I don't think I'm ready for all of this.

Something bumps into my legs, and I turn automatically.

"Oh, excuse me—holy shit!"

I jump back into Bati, whose arms come around to steady us. The large, blobbish thing that basically looks like a giant poop emoji with glowing antennae slinks past me at a surprising quick rate. KJ whimpers, his grip tightening around my neck. His breath is quick beneath my ear. Maybe I should have explained the whole alien thing to him first.

Warble.

"Sir, this young human, he is yours?"

"I want Bati!"

KJ pulls back from me and angles his body up at Bati who plucks him from my arms without a thought and settles him at his side. He leans in, speaking softly to my son for a moment. As he speaks, he reaches into his pocket and pulls out a small wrapped square of the blue candy Ah'dan bought KJ before we left Lyqa. He unwraps it and passes it to my son, who takes it and plops it into his mouth before turning into Bati's shoulder and burying his face. Bati rubs a soothing hand over KJ's back before smiling down at me.

"He is mine," Bati says finally, dragging his eyes back to the Qitoni. The man's membrane lined mouth turns down, but after a short stare-off with Bati, he taps the tablet again.

"May I inspect your visitor's pass?"

Bati reaches into the woven leather pouch hanging from his neck and pulls out a thin square of clear material. The Qitoni takes it from him and lays it over the tablet. A second later, it dissolves, disintegrating onto the screen in a million little dots.

"You will visit (warbled sound) and then the west forests?"

He asks after a few seconds of staring at the screen. Even though the translator provides tone, it's hard to get a read on this dude. The tightness of his face doesn't allow for many facial expressions, so I can't tell if this is standard procedure or if they're giving us the third degree because KJ and I are here.

"My *dahni* would like to visit your recreational parks. Then we will complete our *ta'ani maul* in the west forests," Bati returns.

A low gurgle hums out from somewhere inside the Qitoni. My translator doesn't do anything, and I realize what he just did was the human equivalent of "hmm".

"Welcome to Qiton. The tracking and purchasing features on your citizenship bands will remain activated during your stay. All purchases are suspect to inspection upon departure. Enjoy your stay."

After this warbled declaration, Bati steers me away with a hand at my elbow.

"Dude, that was weird as fuck!" I hiss out, keeping my voice low just in case the Qitoni have spidey-hearing, too.

Bati chuckles. "They take some getting accustomed to. Qitoni are not as similar to humans as we are. She was nice, however."

I stop and blink up at him. "That was a woman?"

"Qitoni are a single gender society. They are all female," Bati replies easily and increases the pressure on my back to get me to start walking again. I resist it and continue to stare up at him.

"Wait, a second. If they are all female, how do they have babies?"

Bati looks nervous. He lowers his head.

"They are a self-populating species, *lehti*. They are also somewhat sensitive about discussing their procreation openly. I can explain later." It's the first time I've heard him speak softly. It's barely audible. I guess if you come from a people that can hear everything, you learn to have a real inside voice.

"Right, my bad." My mouth pulls down in apology. Bati takes my arm again and steers me toward a row of open doors leading outside. Before we step out, I stop again. Bati pauses, too, staring down at me patiently.

"Are you okay, my *lehti*?"

I take a deep breath. "No, I'm fine. Maybe not exactly fine. I'm a bit nervous. I guess I wasn't expecting all of this. I just kind of need to know what's waiting for us outside those doors."

He pulls me against him. I'm surprised when his hand slides over my ass and holds me in a gentle grip. Bati can be kind of handsy when he wants.

"Tiani, do you think I would bring you here if it was unsafe? Do you think I would bring my *dahni* here if it was unsafe? You must get used to being in the universe. Things will be strange. Some things will be dangerous, but that is for me to worry about. And you should know that I would never put you in harm's way if I could help it."

"Okay." My voice shakes. The pressure of his hand is making everything below my waist tingle.

"Now, on Earth, you have oceans, yes?" He pats my ass and pulls his hand away.

"What, uh, yeah."

"The Qitoni are an aquatic people. So, if you have ever been in the ocean on Earth, it will look like that."

"Oh, like the beach?"

He tilts his head to the side, his eyes shifting up. He does this when his translator provides information on English words.

"Perhaps. It will be like being in the ocean."

* * *

I'm really going to have to teach Bati more about Earth and about context in the human language.

"See, my *lehti,* it is like being in the ocean." His smile is wide as he squints up into the bring pink sun overhead.

Strike that, I'm really going to have to listen more carefully when he tells me things. He did say *in* the ocean and not *at* the ocean, and as I look around, that's exactly what it looks like. Like someone tossed me overboard and I've sunken down into a coral reef. Except...there's no water.

The scene in front of me is straight out of something from a nature show back home crossed with that movie where the kids shrink themselves into tiny people and run around their backyard.

Huge, flat, seaweed trees line the streets. When we step from the hard surface of the transport center, my feet shift, sinking into the soft ground. Startled, I lose my balance and reach out to steady myself on Bati's arm.

"Do not be scared. The ground is soft because it lives." At my panicked look, Bati shakes his head. "No, it is the earth of this planet. I do not know the word, but my translator is providing the term *sponge*. Is this correct?"

I look down at my feet. The ground beneath me is a burnt orange color. All across the surface are holes of various sizes. I lift to my toes and bounce. The ground gives way slightly with a moist squish. It's almost like being on a trampoline. As I continue to bounce, liquid seeps from the ground and soaks into my thin canvas shoes.

"Is that water?"

"It is. This planet has a hydro core."

"That means it runs on water?"

"It is a host organism of an aquatic nature. The Qitoni live in it as the dominant parasites."

"Wait, you mean the planet is like, alive, alive?"

"It is an instinctual conscious being, yes."

"Uh, okay, and what does that mean? Is it going to open up its mouth and eat us?"

I've stopped bouncing. In fact, I've stopped moving all together. The image of a large, gaping mouth opening up to swallow us down fills me with a paralyzing terror. Bati laughs and pulls me into his side, making me squeal. This doesn't feel like the time to be making sudden movements.

"Tiani, I have told you that there is nothing to fear here. The planet is not conscious in the way you are thinking, but it is responsive. It will defend itself in the ways that it can. However, the Qitoni have existed in symbiotic harmony without issue for many millions of years. You can move freely."

I exhale a shaky breath and take a step forward onto the squishy, moist earth.

"No, not there. That's its eye!" KJ shouts.

I yelp and jump back. My eyes fly to the ground where my foot landed, but it looks like the rest of the surface. There is no giant eye staring up at me. Beside me, Bati and KJ burst into a fit laughter. I turn and narrow my eyes on them. For someone who was quivering in fear a moment ago, KJ's bounced back well enough. Little monster.

Bati's nearly bent over. His deep, melodic laugh washes over me like a warm wave. I don't think I've ever heard him laugh before. His smooth, blue-black face is transformed by his wide grin. He looks young and sweet. It makes me want to kiss him.

I snap out of my trance and strike out with one of my fists to catch Bati with a playful punch to the arm. "You guys are buttheads, you know that? Don't scare me."

Bati chuckles one last time before holding his hand out to me. "Take my hand. That way, if anything unexpected happens, I will be right there to save you."

* * *

BATI

"Can your youngling play with us?" The Qitoni girl at the front of the small group before us stares up at me with wide, swirling silver eyes.

Her scent is excited, as are the other children's in the group. This is probably the first time any of them have seen a human child. The girl's tight skin keeps her excitement from showing even as the membranous flaps of her mouth pull across her face in what I realize is a smile.

"I think he would be happy to play with you," I tell her. KJ regards our exchange with quiet interest. He can't understand us. I did not think to fit him with a translator, but these things don't matter with children.

The large playground in front of us is filled with mostly Qitoni girls and a few species of children from nearby planets. The open space features moss-covered hills, bridges, and play beds. In the center of the play area is a large, hollowed sea willow. Holes cut into the twisting, green trunk allow children to poke their heads through. Most of the children are in the tree and the sandpit. Qitoni children are known for their ability to make intricate sculptures from the fine, black sand. At the moment, a group are working hard on a recreation of a native sea creature.

Tiani shifts closer to me on the other side of KJ, sandwiching him between our legs. She smells nervous. Her scent is tangy and sharp in my nose.

"I—uh, maybe he's not ready—"

"Let's play!" KJ leaps from between us and bolts in the direction of the sea willow. When he's a few feet away, he turns and waves for the group of children to follow. They race after him, catching up just as he reaches the tree.

"KJ, wait!" Tiani takes a step after them, but I stop her with a careful arm across her chest.

"He will be okay, Tiani."

"Oh my god, this is so hard!" she groans, pressing her hands to the sides of her face. "I don't want him to be scared."

I follow her gaze to where KJ is waving gleefully at us from one of the observation holes in the tree.

"He did not smell afraid, and it is clear he is enjoying himself."

"That kid, man." Tiani shakes her head as KJ runs in a circle with one of the Qitoni girls before collapsing to the soft turf in a fit of giggles.

"He is a wonderful, tolerant boy. It is an admirable trait to have so young. It speaks much to your efforts in raising him."

Her mouth turns up, and her skin brightens. She is embarrassed?

"I guess, I should practice what I preach more. I've been told I'm not the nicest."

"You are beautiful. Inside and out," I tell her because it's true. Our gazes lock for a moment before she chuckles and clears her throat, looking off to the side again.

"So, what exactly do we do for this *ta'ani*majig?"

We're sitting on a moss patch at the edge of the playground on the vibrant banks of Qiton's southwest seas. The scenery is alive and lush. Thick beds of violet moss cover the flat grounds. The feathery soft blades are moist as is all of Qiton's aquatic landscape. Tiani reaches beyond the element-resistant blanket I spread out to protect our clothing and runs her hands through the fluttering blades. I observe her profile as she watches KJ play with the group of Qitoni children a few yards away. Most of her is covered by the thin, gauze fabric of the dress I had made for her before we left Lyqa, but I can still see most of her face. The smooth brown skin glistens with a thin sheen of moisture from the damp air. It reminds me of how her skin looked after we joined, and it triggers an inconvenient tightening in my crotch. I shift and will my first heart to slow down.

"Ta'ani maul," I finally answer. My voice is tense. "It is a kind of game. Probably more suited for children, although some of the more advanced adventures can be quite elaborate."

"Elaborate how?"

"Do not worry, my *lehti*." I take the liberty of smoothing my hand down her spine. Even through the material, the heat of her body warms me all the way to my soul. "The one I have chosen for us is very simple. We have a list of fairly common items to collect. They can be retrieved in a central location. It may not be very exciting for us, but I think our *dahni* will enjoy it."

She stares at me with her head cocked to the side.

"What does that mean, *dahni*? The translator supplies something, but I think it's wrong."

"It is not incorrect. It means 'son'." I wait for her expression to turn. It doesn't. Instead, she tilts her head ever further in question.

"You've been calling him your son?"

I don't respond right away because I don't know how to. She waits for an answer, so I gather my thoughts and face her, finally.

"There are some things I have not explained to you that perhaps I should have," I begin.

"About the whole *leht* thing?" she replies, startling me with her candor.

"Yes, about the *leht*."

She looks away, and a faint scent of sadness emanates from her. "I'm sorry I treated you so badly, before. I didn't want to know on Earth. I mean, I knew there was something between us. I could feel it. Here." She presses her hand between her breasts where I'm sure her heart beats as quickly as mine. "Since KJ's father left us, I've had a hard time being close to men," she admits, and her sadness shifts to shame. It makes my skin twitch. She has nothing to be ashamed of.

"The *leht* is a biological function of my first heart. It lays dormant until Lyqa men meet the one they are meant for. The moment it is triggered, it beats only for that person, to serve that person, to protect that person, to—love that person."

"So, you have to be with the person you choose? What if you don't want that person? What if that person doesn't want you?"

I swallow hard around the pain that crowds my chest at her words. I know it is too much to hope she isn't speaking of us. "Tiani, I have not forgotten what you said on Earth. I do not have hope to change your mind, and I am not trying to force you to accept something that is not in your nature. I will not lie and say that I do not feel a deep attachment to you that is partially based on my first heart, but also the fact that you are a beautiful, intelligent, charming woman."

"Charming?"

My shoulder hitches. "When you want to be."

She snorts and looks away. "I'm a jerk. I was a jerk to you, and I didn't have to be. You shouldn't want to be with me."

She smells like despair. She fumbles with the moss, keeping her head turned away. I can't help it. I want to see her eyes. I cradle her cheek with my hand and turn her to face me.

"You are human, my *lehti*. You are allowed to be hurt and scared and even unpleasant at times. I know your heart. I *feel* your heart. It beats with mine, here," I tap over my right chest muscle. She looks down to where my hand rests.

"What do you mean?"

"I mean, that you are my *lehti*. The woman of my heart. We are tied through our heartbeats. Whenever we are near, our hearts will sync. You may have noticed."

She presses her hand between her breasts. "Is that what

I've been feeling? Why my heart has been beating so loudly since the night we were together?"

I take her hand from her chest and place it over mine. I put my other hand where hers was between her breasts. "Listen."

She tilts her head in focus. After a moment, her eyes widen.

"Oh my god, that's really intense." Her scent clouds over with anxiety, and I know she is panicking with the weight of my revelation.

"I do not tell you this to pressure you into loving me back, Tiani. I understand why you feel as you do, and I would have you know that I love you. I will always love you and KJ. And anyway, I can be of assistance to you, I will."

Chapter 10

TIANI

I don't know how to respond to Bati's declaration, but something warm and nice rushes through me at his words. It makes me lean in and press my lips to his. His lips flinch, but after a moment, he kisses me back. Taking hold of my arms, he turns into me, deepening the kiss. His tongue flicks through my mouth, and I moan around it.

"My friends are leaving."

Bati and I jump apart and turn to KJ who's standing out of breath in front of us. His eyes are wide with excitement. I'm happy that he's had a good time. This kid is special. He really is.

"Wha—what, baby?" My heart is beating fast, too fast. I realize now that it can't be my heart. It's Bati's. The beat is a heavy thump over my own.

"My friends said it's high time. They have to go." He points back to the playground where Qitoni mothers are ushering their daughters to waiting transports. The Qitoni girl from earlier waves frantically at KJ as her mother lifts her into their pod. I turn to Bati.

"High time?"

He laughs. "High tide. The sea is coming in from the east."

He points to the ground. Cloudy, black water rises at the base of the moss, seeming to come up from the ground itself. It spills over the edge of the blanket and soaks into my dress. I jump to my feet and the soft soles of my canvas Qitoni sandals slosh in the forming puddle.

"Is this normal?"

"It's the beach!" KJ jumps into the puddle and squeals. He dances around in a circle, flicking up handfuls of water. I do my best to dodge the spray. Bati smiles and motions for us to get off the blanket.

"It will rise for the next few hours. We are safe. If it gets too high, we can swim." He folds the blanket, compressing the plastic-like material until it's a square small enough to fit in his palm. He tucks this back into his pack. He's so focused on his task that he doesn't see the face I make.

"Um, I can't swim."

Bati's head snaps up. He scowls and plants his hands at his waist. "How is this possible? Earth is seventy-five percent water."

"I never had a chance to learn," I fess up, a little embarrassed by how silly it sounds. "Chicago doesn't really have a beach. It's just a lake. I just kind of wade around in it. I never really needed to learn."

Bati huffs out a disappointed breath but steps close to me and pulls me against him, pressing his nose to mine. "*Ma'h qitah*, my *lehti*. I did not mean to shame you. We will remedy this. I will teach you. It will be fun."

I imagine playing around in the water with him. It's not a bad picture. In fact, it's kind of hot.

"Ew, why are you guys kissing so much?"

I chuckle nervously and try to push away from Bati, but he doesn't let me go far before his arms lock. He turns to KJ and raises an inquisitive brow. "And how about you, my *dahni*, can you swim?"

"Like a fish!" KJ drops to his belly and starts to kick his legs in the ankle-deep water. His arms arch through the moss, one after the other. "Cupcake hands! Cupcake hands!"

Bati laughs but looks down at me in confusion.

"Cupcake hands helps him remember how to stroke properly."

Bati nods. "Ah, I see. You have very good form, my *dahni,* but we must leave if we are to make it to our campsite before the high tide comes." He turns a playfully disapproving glance at me and scoops KJ from the ground. My son doesn't stop his swimming demonstration. His legs and arms continue to flail about in the air.

"I'm a fish, *Apha*!"

We freeze. My eyes go wide at the same moment as Bati's. KJ, oblivious to the gravity of what he's said, continues to laugh and wiggle in Bati's hands.

Holy shit. I don't have to ask what that word means. My translator kicks in, and there is no mistaking the words that whisper through my head after KJ's shout. *Beloved father*.

"I will instruct him not to call me that if you wish," Bati says softly beside me. I pretend like I don't hear him and continue to look down where I'm stepping.

My kid thinks that Bati is his dad or something. I don't even know what to do with that. Partly because I'm too embarrassed that he's never known his real dad in any meaningful way, and also because when he said it, it didn't feel wrong. Slowly but surely, whether I realized it or not, over the past few days I have come to see our threesome as a family. It happened so quickly. It was almost like we just clicked together and I didn't even realize it.

We're wading through the water on the way to our campsite. It's knee deep now. The gauze fabric of my dress floats around me, tangling in my legs with each step. I kick my legs up, trying to unravel it.

"I don't want to diss Qitoni fashion, but this is the most impractical design ever!" I lash my foot out in frustration, sending up a spray of water. In addition to trying to navigate the rising tide, the various moss and plant life is obstructed by the pitch-black water and I keep tripping.

"That is a low tide dress. For strolling and protecting the Qitoni's delicate skin from sun damage. During high tide, they discard their clothing."

I trip again, but right myself. "They walk around naked?"

"They swim without clothing, yes. It is more practical."

He continues walking, but I reach out and take hold of his arm to stop him. The muscles bunch beneath my fingers as he turns to face me. KJ is perched on his shoulders. Bati produced another square of Lyqa taffy from his pocket, and my son is busy covering his face and Bati's red curly hair in neon blue goop. "Wait, they swim? Like the entire time?"

"They are an aquatic species, as I have said. They are similar to…" he looks up as he searches for the English word in his internal translator. "jellyfish, perhaps."

"They're animals?"

"We are all animals," he returns, dryly, and I bend down to flick some water at him, making him laugh.

"You know what I mean."

"Yes, I do. They are an amphibious species. They have evolved in symbiosis with the planet and dwell both on land and in water. Does that satisfy you?"

I focus back on my feet because the way Bati's blue eyes bore into mine is too much. He's so cute. Even more so when he's happy and playful. It makes it harder to fight the attraction that I'm even more aware of since he explained the *leht*.

"We are nearly at the campsite. It is there." He points in the distance to a ginormous yellow tree. The flat top hangs lopsidedly over the trunk. It looks similar to the hollowed tree the kids at the park played in.

"What is that?" I huff out as I struggle to keep up with Bati's long strides. Each step is like walking through quicksand.

"It is a sea willow. Visitors use them as campsites."

Bati stops abruptly and turns to me. I'm about to ask what's wrong, but he wraps his arms around my back and hauls me up against him. My dripping legs dangle above the water.

"Put your legs around my waist."

"Wh-what?" I sputter. I can't think when I'm this close to him. His blue eyes sparkle in the dark of his face, throwing off my senses.

"*Lehti,* I love you, but you are slow. I will carry you the rest of the way. If we must walk at your pace, we will never make it." His mouth curves up, teasingly.

"So, you're going to carry me?" I'm playing coy, but I can't wait to be pressed against his big body.

"I will, unless you are opposed." His nostrils flare, and I know he can smell just how not opposed I am.

I sigh dramatically. "If you must."

He holds me up like I weigh nothing. I check on KJ. He's bent over Bati's head asleep. His blue, sticky hands are clasped under Bati's chin, and his cheek rests in Bati's hair. Bati holds him steady with a hand around his back.

I lift my legs, kicking the flaps of the dress aside, and wrap them around Bati's waist, securing my ankles at his lower back. I fumble with my arms, not knowing where to put them.

"Take hold of KJ. That way, I can hold you while you keep him steady."

I do ask he says. I take KJ's arms, careful not to wake him.

Bati releases him and a second later, his hands slide under my ass, hitching me up against his waist. I gasp as my crotch comes in contact with the unmistakable ridge of Bati's dick. He grunts softly over me.

"I do not want you to fall," he mumbles, but doesn't begin to walk again. He stares down at me, his eyes flickering over my face. I flex my legs, pushing our bodies even closer. Bati's jaw clenches.

"I have packed a small tent for KJ and larger one for us to share." As always, his breath is minty and warm. "Is that acceptable?"

I know what he's asking, and I don't try to hide my eagerness. I flex my legs again, grinding our middles together.

"It is more than acceptable."

The reply is barely out of my mouth before he swoops his head down and mashes his mouth to mine. His thin, slippery tongue sweeps through my mouth, ticking the sensitive roof. We stand kissing for a long while. When he finally pulls away, I'm out of breath. I suck in a deep lungful of air.

"My heart." It's a soft whisper. Barely loud enough for me to hear. His expression is heated, and his erection presses against me.

"I'm glad I'm here with you, Bati." It's getting easier and easier to say these things. I want to say them.

"I am glad you are here with me, Tiani."

He starts walking again, and every movement is a delicious ache that have no interest in getting away from.

BATI

I force my legs to move through the thick water because this isn't the time to indulge in my baser instincts. And while the tightening in my pants makes it difficult to navigate the water comfortably, I know I have to wait until we are alone in our tent to do everything I wish to do at the moment.

We reach the giant sea willow just as the water reaches my waist. The entire journey, my *lehti* has remained quiet. Although her scent grew apprehensive as the water rose higher and higher on our entwined bodies, there was an undercurrent of excitement.

When we get to the base of the willow, I look down at the top of Tiani's head. Now that we are still, I realize she's shaking. The cloudy, black water around us is frigid, and the sun has begun to set. I should have dressed her more properly. A walking dress is not the most appropriate for this time of year, but I could not resist the opportunity to see all of her smooth, brown skin peeking from beneath the sheer fabric. My keen eyesight has been able to detect the dark tips of her nipples through the bodice of her dress, and it has been all I could do to keep myself together.

But now she is cold and I am sure also hungry. I will see to my *lehti* and *dahni*'s dinner as soon as we make camp.

"Release KJ to me and step up onto the trunk," I instruct softly. She raises sleepy eyes to me and lets KJ go once I have taken hold of him. "Feel to the left with your feet. The base of the tree is there."

Tiani kicks her legs to the side and makes contact with the solid base. This tree has been modified for campers. I lift her out of the water and onto the first step that leads up the side of the trunk.

When she is on the base, she reaches out for KJ then pulls back, planting her hands at her hips. A little flush of embarrassment dances beneath her brown skin.

"Boy, how long have you been awake?"

"Long time," KJ proclaims above me. I lift him over my head and turn him around in my hands. He is, in fact, wide awake. He smiles and goes to his mother while I pull myself out of the cold water.

"Um, so do we just go up the side?" She points to the flight of Qitoni made steps, but her eyes keep flicking down my body. The water has made the thin materials of our dress stick to our bodies. Every place her eyes land warms me, and I have to close my eyes to gain control. Tiani's dress has been made even more sheer from the water. Help me.

"Bati?"

I open my eyes. She's looking at me with something of concern.

"I am fine, Tiani. These steps will lead you to our campsite." She looks at me closely for another moment before taking KJ's hand and turning to go up the steps. The trunk of the sea willow is massive and winding. Sea willow bark is known for its sturdy, rock like material. This willow was been dried out from the sun. The petrified structure has no more life, but stands as a safe place for campers during high tide.

As I follow them up the steps, I can't help but linger on the rounded curve of my *lehti*'s behind. Her hips sway seductively as she takes the steps, her movements made only more pronounce by the tired lag in her step. Beside her, KJ hops from step to step, his jerky movements causing his mother to trip.

"KJ, come walk with me," I tell him, and he wastes no time releasing his mother's hand and leaping back into my waiting arms. Tiani only glances back briefly before continuing up the steps. I lift KJ onto my side and reach into the pouch around my neck to pull out the task list for this *ta'ani*. I need a distraction.

"*Dahni*, these are all of the things we need to collect to complete our mission," I exaggerate. There are only four things, a meager amount. Most *ta'ani* have no less than twenty items.

"What does it say? I'm gonna get 'em all!" KJ tosses his

arms into the air, his little fists bunched together in anticipated victory. I laugh and ruffle his head. He reminds me so much of Ah'dan. His curiosity. His surety of self. He is magical and joyful. Tiani has done so well with him.

"This is a *wuor'gi.*" I warble the Qitoni word in my throat.

"Wooooooogie," KJ repeats, pursing his mouth and wavering his voice on the vowel, triggering a soft laugh from Tiani.

"Very good, my *dahni. Wuor'gi.* It is a beautiful multi-colored stone found in the west seas. They are said to bring good fortune to those who keep them."

"What is multi-colored?" KJ asks.

"It means something with a lot of different colors, baby," Tiani huffs out in front of us. We are nearly to the top, but it has been a long trek, and she is low on energy.

"How will we find the woogie?"

"We must look around. We must search for one." I don't mention that the ground where we step is littered with *wuor'gi.* It is a very common stone on Qiton. One could look at the ground at any moment and find one. With the high tide, they are only slightly more difficult to find without diving for them.

"Ugh, finally!" Tiani comes to a halt in front of us and heaves out a deep breath, planting her hands at her lower back. "Dude, I thought you were tryin to kill me. That was crazy."

She takes in another deep breath and steps up onto the flat top of the willow. The branches have long fused to create a tightly woven platform that is safe to stand on. Still, she steps carefully forward, looking down at where her feet land.

"It is safe, Tiani. Western sea willow is one of the strongest materials on Qiton."

She steps more surely onto the platform, making way for me to step up with KJ. I lower him, and he immediately takes off across the platform, his body bent over as he peers closely at the ground.

Apprehension rises in Tiani just as her mouth opens to call after him.

"He is not in danger, *lehti*. You do not need to worry. I would not bring you to a place where harm could come to either of you."

She looks at me guiltily. "I'm sorry. I know you know what you're doing. This is just so different. Black folks don't really do camping, you know?"

This is strange. "I do not know. What keeps humans of your ethnicity from camping?"

She turns to me and laughs, dropping her hands and shaking her head. "That's a joke. We camp, we're just not about putting ourselves in unnecessarily dangerous situations. It's a cultural thing, I guess."

This makes sense. Lyqa, too, enjoy adventure but are not inclined to acts of needless recklessness.

"Do not worry. I do not take chances with my family," I return before I realize what I have said. "I do not mean to imply that we are partnered. I just mean—my brother and your sister are partnered therefore—"

"It's okay. I know what you mean." She looks away, but her cheeks warm brightly. I clear my throat and drop our packs from my back. They fall beside KJ's, which he dropped before running off.

"We should prepare our tents. The sun has begun lowering and the air will cool. In the morning, we can start the *ta'ani*. It should only take a day to complete. I will also give you a swimming lesson in the morning." I pull the thin, element resistant tent from my pack and begin to unfold it.

"What am I supposed to swim in? I didn't exactly pack a swim suit."

"Your clothing is of no matter. I will teach you to float, and if we have time a basic paddle. Much like KJ's cupcake hands."

When I glance up, Tiani is smirking down at me. "If you say so."

Chapter 11

TIANI

"Are your eyes functioning improperly?"

I blink on the side of Bati's blue-black face. I've been staring. I can't help it. I spent the past half hour watching this Lyqa dude in wilderness mode and it's kind of hot. First, he'd propped our tents. I was surprised to find that the same blanket we used at the park opened even further, and with the wave of his hand over a sensor, poofed into a large domed tent. Then he'd pulled a smaller tent from KJ's pack and set it up right next to ours.

He's preparing dinner. I'm useless right now. I wouldn't know what to do with the flat, round pad he slaps on the ground if he told me. I have nothing to do but stare at him. The way the muscles in his arms and back bunch and ripple every time he moves. He doesn't look up after his question and I clear my throat and look away.

"It's 'do you have an eyesight problem'."

"Do you?" He turns to look at me and his blue eyes sparkle.

"Maybe."

His gaze flares briefly before he turns back to the pad. He

waves his hand over it and the center begins to glow. A red ring spreads outward until the entire pad is bright. It's warm from where I sit. Bati pulls a small pouch from his pack and tosses it on top of the heated pad. Almost immediately, it begins to puff up, steam shooting from a small hole in the top.

"Wow, that's so cool. Is the food in there?"

He nods. A second later, he slides the pouch from the pad and waves his hand over it again. The red ring immediately disappears. He reaches out to pick it up, and instinctively, I grab his arm to stop him.

"Don't burn yourself!"

Bati chuckles and eases his arm from my hand. Before I can stop him, he slaps his hand down on the pad. Nothing happens.

"It is okay, my *lehti*. The heat is gone."

"Oh."

He puts the pad back in his pack and passes me a long handled three-pronged fork.

"KJ, it is time to eat. Come, little one."

KJ drops the blocks he's playing with and turns into the circle, taking the fork I hold out to him. Bati pulls the sides of the pouch apart and steam plumes out to reveal a pile of vegetables. They're glazed in some kind of dark sauce. A spicy, sweet smell wafts up between us, and my stomach grumbles. I'm starving.

I reach in and spear one of the veggies then hold it out for KJ. He immediately scrunches up his nose and turns his face away.

"Bleh, I hate carrots."

I laugh and pull the fork to my mouth, taking a bite. It does taste a bit like a carrot, except it's sweeter. More like a sweet potato. I make a show of chewing enthusiastically and hold the fork back out to him.

"No, it's yummy, baby. It tastes like sweet potato pie."

"It looks like a carrot." He holds his mouth tightly closed.

"KJ, I will give you *sawa* if you do not like it, but you must try it first." Bati holds up a round, furry fruit. It kind of looks like a large purple kiwi.

"Okay. Ah!"

This kid is never this easy when it comes to veggies, but one word from Bati and he's ready to try anything. I'd be salty about it, but honestly, anything to get him to eat is fine with me.

I fork the food into his mouth and he chews for a second, bobbing his head thoughtfully like he's really considering the taste. All of a sudden, his mouth drops open and I cup my hand beneath his chin just before the glob of veggies hits his shirt.

"KJ! You almost messed up your shirt, kid."

"K," Bati gives a pretty convincing laying down the law look. "If you do not like something, you spit it discreetly into your hand and give it to me or your *amha,* do you understand?"

KJ's face shifts down in exaggerated shame, and you could knock me over with a feather. Well, I'll be.

"Sorry," he mumbles.

"Good. Now you can have the *sawa,* but you must also eat some of the *q'ish*. I suspect it was not as bad as you pretend."

KJ takes a deep breath and huffs it out. "It wasn't that yucky. I just wanted banana fruit." He takes the fruit Bati holds out. The moment it hits his hand, a big grin breaks out over his face, and he takes a bite, spraying juice all over his shirt, anyway.

Bati's eyes slide back into his head in an exaggerated eye roll.

"Younglings," he mumbles, shaking his head.

We continue eating. KJ moves back to his blocks as he eats

his fruit, and I take another vegetable and plop it into my mouth. They really are quite good. They don't look like carrots. More like yellow broccoli. Crunchy but soft. The glaze tastes almost like apricots and vinegar.

"You're good with him," I admit after a moment. Bati's eyes flick to me and then away.

"Amina has told me this. I have always had a way with children. Unlike Kwarq, I am not uncomfortable with being firm."

I snort. He's right. Kwarq might look like a tough guy, but he's a big ol' softie. Amina has him wrapped around every last one of her fingers. Even though they are twins, I kind of like that Bati is more of a hard ass, and yet, he's still just as sweet, just as considerate and caring as his brother.

"I bet you're excited to be an uncle."

"I am. It is always exciting to have new life, new family to love and care for." His expression is wistful.

I take another bite of food and chew slowly. This is the first time we've talked about ourselves. I find I want to know more.

"What about you? Do you think you'll have kids of your own?"

The second the words leave my mouth, I know it's a mistake. Bati stares at me for a long moment and my heart clenches at the sadness in his expression. After a moment, he smiles, but it's forced and pained.

"I do not think that is part of my future, but I am happy to enjoy the children of my brothers—and KJ, while he is here." He glances over to my son and his expression warms, making my throat tighten.

"I really appreciate how much you've cared for him."

"Of course. My *leht* is not just to you. It is to every part of you, including KJ. I am as drawn to him as a son as I am to you as—" he pauses and looks away. "I care very much for him. I consider him my own, my *dahni*. My—son. I love him very much." He looks back to me and his blue eyes shine with emotion before he blinks, neutralizing his expression. "I will clean up our dinner. Would you like to put KJ to bed, or shall I?"

I take the task of bed time just to end the conversation. I don't need Lyqa senses to realize this is an awkward moment. I also don't need Bati to tell me that if he wanted to have kids it would probably have to be with me. Surprisingly, the idea of being with him isn't the worst thing I can think of. It's actually the nicest thought I've had in a long time. Like always, I want to say this to him, but now isn't the right time. Instead, I grab KJ's pack and start looking through it for something for him to wear to bed.

Bati has thought of everything. Inside KJ's little bag is a toothbrush, towels for washing, and several changes of clothes, including KJ's favorite race car pajamas. The kid is tired. Not five minutes after I get him ready and settled for bed, he's already asleep, huddled beneath a thermal blanket in his tent, a Lyqa block clutched in his hand.

When I come out of KJ's tent, Bati is swishing something from a canteen around his mouth. He walks to the edge of the platform and spits, wiping his mouth as he turns.

"Would you like to clean your teeth?"

He walks back to me and holds out the container. I take it and bring it to my lips. It's not a toothbrush, but I guess it's better than nothing. I tilt it to my mouth, and instead of water, a thick liquid slides between my lips. I gag, clamping my mouth tight in an effort to keep from spitting, and turn wide eyes up at Bati.

He's laughing slightly. "Do not worry. It is a bio-wash. Microorganisms will remove the particles of food from between your teeth and freshen your breath."

Holy shit. Bio-wash? Organisms? Did this dude just tell me that I'm holding a bunch of bugs in my mouth? Rushing over to the edge of the platform, I spit the liquid out, gathering mouthfuls of saliva and spitting over and over.

"Dude, warn a girl before you give her a mouth full of bugs, okay?"

He chuckles again. "I apologize. I should have realized that would be strange for you. I packed this as well." He holds out a toothbrush. I snatch it and start scrubbing at my teeth and tongue. Bati hands me another bottle and I hesitate to take it.

"It is just water," he assures me.

It is. I swish it around my mouth and spit over the side. When I turn back to the camp, Bati is standing by our tent. He has removed his shirt. A pair of thin, sleeping shorts rest low on his hips. I swallow. His eyes flick down to the region of my throat. Yeah, I bet he heard that.

"Are you ready for bed, Tiani?"

BATI

"Uh, yeah. I'm ready."

She smells nervous. I can hear the muscles of her throat work loudly as she swallows. I have been waiting for this moment all day. The opportunity for privacy. A moment to be close to her without reserve.

I hold open the flap to the tent and she crawls in, moving quickly to one side of the blanket I have laid out. I check KJ's tent one final time before ducking inside and sealing the flap behind me.

"Will he be okay out there by himself?"

"He will be fine, Tiani." I tap my earlobe. "Spidey-hearing, remember? If he even breathes uncomfortably, I will hear it. Also, our hearts are bound. If he is in danger, I will feel it."

Her eyes widen on my face. "Your heart is bound to his,

too? How?"

I settle down in front of her on the pallet and take her hands, bringing them to my mouth.

"I have told you that I am *leht* to you both. You are of my heart, but he is also. I am bound to you as a mate, and I am bound to him as a father. Do not question it. Despite our inability to be together, I am happy for it."

"Damn, dude." She extracts one of her hands from mine and brings it up to my face, cradling my jaw. The warmth of her skin goes straight through me, and my body reacts, sending a surge of desire to my cock. I start to rise beneath my sleeping shorts, and Tiani's gaze lingers on my waist before she pulls back from me and lifts her layered top over her head.

"Come here," she whispers. The anticipation rolling off of her is potent in the enclosed space. She wants me, and I want her. I want her more intensely than ever before.

She tosses her shirt to the side and I fix on the dark, straining peaks of her breasts. It has only been two days since I was last with her, but it feels like an eternity, and I need to be close to her, to feel her. Yet something within me hesitates.

"You do not have to join with me because I am bound to you. I did not bring a single tent to force you into my bed." I reach out and run the back of one hand over the firm curve of her breast. She is so soft, so silky. Every bit of her is brown and even. The only variation in color is her nipples, her black, curly hair and the matching patch that covers her pussy.

"I don't want to sleep with you because you are *leht* to me, Bati. I want to sleep with you because despite what an asshole I've been, I like you. I really like you."

She smiles shyly up at me, but I'm too stunned to move.

"Tiani?" Her name sticks in my throat. I try to swallow around it, but the knot does not want to move. I cannot believe it.

She rises to her knees before wrapping her arms around my shoulders and pulling me into the fragrant valley of her breasts. "I said, I like you."

I rest my chin against her chest. She's smiling. Her scent is light and sweet. The edge of resistance I can usually sense is gone. I dare to believe she has accepted the *leht*, that she has accepted me.

"Are you going to leave me hanging?"

I frown. "I do not know what that means."

"Well, when someone says they like you, it's kind of a thing to say it back."

Lyqa fast, I spin us around and lower her to the pallet. I nuzzle the sweet skin of her chest and she moans beneath me.

"I am quite fond of you, my *lehti*, if I have not made it obvious. Had you never grown fond of me, I would have loved you until I returned to the stars."

"And now that I do like you?" She smells nervous again. Does she think I will ever let her go?

"Now that you like me, I am the happiest being in the universe."

Her fingers dance across my chest nervously. "But is it okay that I'm not really sure about the whole love thing? I mean I like you. I do. I think I've liked you since I first met you, but I just don't know. It seems a little early to talk about love, you know?"

She smells guilty. I do not like it. "It is okay, my *lehti*. However, you feel for me is enough. I do not expect more, and if in the future, your affection grows for me, I will be glad for it, but I do not expect it."

"So, it's cool if we just kind of go with the flow?"

"It is cool."

Her tension lifts away. "So, now that we officially like each other, what should we do?" Her finger trails along the side of my face. When it gets close to my mouth, I catch it gently with my teeth, flicking my tongue out to taste her.

"Now, at this very moment, I am going to make you scream." I dive between her breasts, pressing kisses along every bit of flesh I can, making her shriek and giggle. When I swirl my tongue around one tight nipple, she moans and arches into my mouth.

"We have to be quiet," she whispers around another moan. She tastes like the salty air of Qiton. I cover the straining peak and suck gently before releasing her with a wet plop. She gasps and pushes my head away.

"Do not worry. No one will hear us. When you come from a species with hearing as good as Lyqas', you learn to perfect discretion technology," I point to the wall of the tent.

"No one can hear us outside?"

I shake my head.

"Then how will you hear KJ?"

"Our tent is shielded from the outside, but not the inside. His is not at all. Do not worry."

A slow smile spreads across her face as she looks up at me. "So, I can be as loud as I want?"

I rise so that our noses touch and press a kiss to her soft lips.

"You may be as loud you wish, Tiani."

I lower my mouth back to her breast and trace the tip with my tongue. Her soft gasps echo through my ears as I taste her. I lap at her smooth flesh. The firm mounds of her breasts bounce against my tongue.

"Bati!"

I have never heard a more pleasing sound than Tiani gasping my name in pleasure. I close my mouth over her nipple and she moans loudly, arching up from the blanket. I move to her other breast, pressing feather light kisses before suckling firmly against her.

"Bati, please! I can't—"

"I understand."

There is an urgency emanating from her that matches my own desperate desire. It has been too long since I've held her, and as much as I would like to take my time, to lick every inch of her, taste all of her sweet places, I want to be inside of her more.

I push my sleeping shorts down my hips and free my cock. It's heavy and so hard that I ache. Tiani begins to pull at her complicated Qitoni skirt with little success. I help her, unwinding the strips of fabric until they lay in a pile around her soft, brown body.

"You are beautiful," I whisper when she is finally bared for me. Her long, toned legs lay open, and the glistening petals of pussy call to me. I dip my head and drag my tongue through her folds, savoring her sweetness, the purity of her arousal.

"Oh my god!"

She sounds pained. I would have my *lehti* sound satisfied. I kiss her one last time and move up her body, allowing no space between us. She opens for me, spreading her thighs wide, and my cock meets the heat of her center, pressing into the tight sheath until I reach her womb, and every part of me is surrounded by her warmth.

"*Hu'l*!" The Lyqa word slips past my lips before I can stop it.

"Bati, you swore!"

My eyes are pressed tight from the sheer bliss of being joined with my *lehti* again. I open them to find Tiani looking up at me with a shocked expression.

"I do not know what this word 'swore' means," I tell her as I ease from her body and press back in a firm, deep stroke.

"Ah—it means—mm, that you said a bad word. Oh my god!"

Her words are stunted as I increase the force of my thrusts. She feels too good. Better than before, and the first time in my *lehti* was the best feeling of my life. Her passage grips me tightly. I raise my hips and flex them down hard, pushing past her resistance again and again. Her little mewling moans get louder and louder until my ears ache from her screams.

"Do you like it, my *lehti*?"

"Yes!"

I lift away from the warmth of her breasts, needing to see her. The short, curly hairs around her forehead are slick with sweat. They form little half-moons about her face that make her look celestial and fantastic. Her dark, nearly black eyes are bottomless pools beneath heavy lids. Her full lips part as she gasps out her pleasure, those tiny human teeth peek from between them. I flick out my tongue, swirling it through her mouth, and she moans lustily, catching my tongue and sucking gently.

"I love kissing you," she murmurs when we part. Her scent is colored with awe.

"You do not find my tongue to be strange? Uncomfortable?"

"Hell no, I like everything about you."

I slow my hips and press a soft kiss to her lush lips.

"Do you have a favorite part?"

She licks across my bottom lip, triggering a round of deep thrusts before I am able to calm myself again.

"Tell me, Tiani. What is your favorite part?"

She's so wet. The sounds of her arousal make it hard to think about anything but releasing. I hold her knees wide, sinking deeper. Her face lights in surprise as she stretches around me. Every nerve along my cock surges to life as her walls constrict and spasm along my length.

"Everything!" she finally yelps as I continue to work her in quick, deep thrusts.

"Everything is not one part. I would know. Tell me." I hitch my hips up, striking along the underside of her passage and she screams.

"Bati!" Her body jerks and spasms beneath me as an orgasm rips through her. I work her through it, gliding into her pussy at an easy pace until the tension leaves her body. When she stills, her chest heaving, I slip from her inside of her.

"You didn't finish." Her head is raised from the floor. She looks at me with concern.

"I did not. Turn to your knees."

My cock throbs in front of me. The tip is leaking a steady stream of semen. I am close to release, but I have not had enough of my *lehti*. I need more.

Tiani's eyes flare, and she rolls over, presenting her curved behind to me. She eases up to her knees, and the slick slit of her pussy spreads before me.

I don't wait. I raise to my knees behind her and press back in until every inch of me is pulsing through her.

"Mmm," Tiani lowers her head and breathes deeply.

"Is it too much?" I can sense the tension is her body. Her tissue swells tightly around my cock. She cannot take me for much longer.

"No, it feels good." She dips her back, easing me in even deeper.

"*Hu'l*! Tiani, have mercy." My release lingers at the edge of my pleasure. I begin to move, hammering into her, eager to get the that place. With each plunge of my cock into her tight depths, my balls tighten, until they are pressed so close to my body that they ache.

"Bati, come!"

I have been working her hard. Her upper body is pressed to the pallet. Her hands fist in the blanket, and her sharp cries ring out in the room with each flex of my hips. My movements are a blur. The pleasure rioting through me reaches a peak just as Tiani hisses a deep breath of air through her teeth and begins to shake with a second orgasm.

"*Lehti*!" I come with a fierce growl, pressing so far into her that we both collapse to the ground. For long moments, my cock pulses stream after stream of semen at her womb until I have nothing left.

I drop my weight to her back, unable to hold myself up anymore. I'm drained, while at the same time, the most exhilarating energy courses through every one of my cells.

We lay in silence for a moment. The only sound is that of our breath huffing out. Tiani shifts beneath me, and I lift to my elbows revealing her sweat slicked form beneath me.

"I did not mean to crush you, Tiani."

"Mm, I'm good."

I nuzzle the moist space between her back, flicking out my tongue to taste the beads of salty sweat.

"I would have you feeling well."

She sighs contentedly and I catch the edges of her smile. "I am more than well. I am awesome."

"Are you awesome enough for more?"

I do not know what is wrong with me, but I have not had enough. If anything, the strange energy has given me a renewed desire. My cock is still thick and rigid inside of her despite having released.

I press forward and she moans, leaning back against me as my hips start to move again.

Chapter 12

TIANI

Something jolts me awake. I lurch up out of my sleep and immediately regret it. My entire body protests. My thighs ache. My breasts are tender and sore. My pussy feels like it's been pounded to death.

I experience a moment of confusion, until I remember where I am. Alien planet number two. With Bati and KJ. Shared tent. Amazing sex.

I'm alone. The therma-blanket is tangled around my waist, and the pallet is cool and damp where Bati's cum dripped out of me. I scoot over until I get to a dry spot and press my hands to the insides of my thighs to massage the tension out of my legs.

"Ahh!" KJ's voice shrieks out just before I hear a loud splash outside and then silence. I wait a second, listening for some further movement, for his voice again or Bati's. I continue to wait. Finally, too much time passes, and I climb to my knees as panic overtakes me.

"KJ?" I wait. Nothing.

"Bati?" Again, everything outside the tent is silent.

I start fighting to get out of the tent. The walls are thin, but they're sturdy and resist against my frantic fingers. I finally find the opening and pull it back before tumbling out onto the warm platform of the sea willow. The surface is smooth, but the little holes across the top dig into my knees. I jump to my feet and rush toward the edge. A foot below the platform, the water is quiet. Fear grips me. My heart thumps like it's about to burst out of my chest.

"KJ!" My voice is a panicked scream. My eyes shift over the dark, gently rolling water. A large ripple fans out from a spot a few feet from the edge. Several bubbles appear from the murky depths and break the surface. Without thinking, I drop to the side of the platform and begin to lower myself into the water. It's warm as it laps around my ankles and then my calves. I begin to shake as my thighs slide over the edge. I take a deep breath and try to think of all the things the water safety instructors taught my son. *Cupcake hands, cupcake hands,* I chant in my head.

"Be easy, little one."

Someone's arm comes around and catches me just as my hips sink into the water. I don't recognize the voice, but it's male. The accent isn't Lyqa. It's deeper and oddly even. The English words sound monotone, almost robotic. Whoever he is, he isn't going to stop me from saving my son. I struggle against his hold, looking down at the large, veiny—silver?—arm.

"Let me go! My son—"

Just then, the surface of the water breaks, and first KJ's and then Bati's smiling faces appear. My breath whooshes out along with a relieved sob.

"Mommy, I found a woogie!" KJ holds his hand up above the water. Gripped between his fingers is what looks like a flat marble.

"Bati, what the fuck!"

I words burst from my mouth, and the smiles drop from

both of their faces. KJ's eyes widen, and I know what he's going to say before he even opens his mouth.

"I know I cursed, KJ, okay?" I shout louder than I mean to and stand up to hold a hand over the edge. "Out! Get out of the water now!"

Bati's expression shifts to concern but he treads the short way to the platform and hands KJ up. I pull my son from his hands and push past whoever was standing behind me to carry him to the middle of the platform where I set him down to check him over. Rivulets of dark water stream down his face. He watches me warily.

"Are you mad at me, Mommy?"

KJ's tiny voice breaches my panic-stricken brain, and I drop down to my knees, exhaling loudly. He's fine.

"She is not upset with you, my *dahni*. She is upset with me. I should not have taken you into the water without her permission. *Ma'h qitah.*" Bati drops to his knees beside us and pulls us both against his sides. He nuzzles my head, pressing a kiss into my curls.

"I'm sorry I yelled at you. I just panicked. I heard a splash, and I wasn't fully awake. I thought you fell in. I was calling you."

Bati angles his head so he's looking straight at me. "I came up as soon as I heard you calling."

"I was calling for a long time!"

"Were you still inside the tent?"

"Yeah, I was sleeping. I heard the splash and I jumped up and called you!"

Bati nuzzles my temple, pressing light kisses. "I would not ignore you, ever, my *lehti*, but the tent is discreet."

Right. That's why I could be as loud as I wanted last night. Embarrassment washes over me.

"Oh, my god. I forgot. I'm so stupid. Sorry."

"Do not apologize. Even though you are confident in our

dahni's ability to swim, I should not have taken him diving without speaking to you first."

A groan rumbles up from my throat that I can't stop.

"Dude, you took my four-year-old son diving?"

He beams. "Actually, I had to teach him to dive first, but he is a very quick learner, much like a fish as he has said. We were able to reach the bottom of the sea on the third try."

KJ's head nods proudly. I know Bati thinks he's impressing me right now, but, really, diving with a four-year-old? I want to be pissed, but he's so oblivious to my annoyance that I find myself just shrugging.

"Look, that's great, but no more diving unless mommy is awake and there to tell you not to do it, okay?"

"Of course, my *lehti*."

"Okay, mommy."

They both stare at me, waiting. I glance between their somewhat awkward expressions and laugh.

"Well let me see this darn wookie you guys almost gave me a heart attack over."

Bati pulses bright pink and KJ slaps his hands over his mouth to smother a laugh.

"What?"

Bati's ears are damn near glowing as he leans close. "Perhaps, you would like to inspect our find after you have had a chance to clothe yourself."

"What?"

I follow his pointed gaze. I'm naked. Like stark naked. In my rush to get to KJ, I scrambled out of the tent with nothing on. I cross my hands over my breasts and slap a palm between my legs, while at the same time, huddling into as tight a ball as I can.

"Bati, get me something. A shirt. Anything!"

"This may be of some use."

That same strange, monotone voice sounds out just as a

cloth falls across my shoulders. I waste no time pulling it securely around me. I wrap it over my chest and tuck the ends under my arms. Black girls don't blush, but I feel my face warm beneath everyone's gaze.

"Thank you," I mumble without looking up. I'm too embarrassed.

"You are most welcome," the voice replies, and the platform shakes slightly as he walks away.

"What is he?"

I keep my voice as low as possible. One thing I've learned about aliens is that they all seem to have really good hearing...and sight...and speed. It doesn't stop me from being nosey about our new addition to the campsite.

Bati said he arrived some time during the night. He heard him and left the tent to greet him, and once he had assured himself the guy was okay, went back to bed. I can't imagine what about this dude could lull anyone back to sleep.

He's...different. Bati and his family—all Lyqa really—aren't much different than humans. Yeah, they're bigger and the mixture of their features can be strange, confusing even, but aside from the really long tongues, they don't offer much in the way of *alien*.

This dude isn't Qitoni weird or giant shit emoji weird, but he definitely couldn't walk around Earth the way Bati and Kwarq did. Not unless there was a cosplay convention happening in town.

He isn't that much taller than Bati and his brothers, and like Lyqas, he fits his height. There is none of the awkwardness that is common with really tall humans. But he isn't just tall. He's big all over. Everything looks super-sized in a way that appears too natural to be anything but other-worldly. One of his arms looks about the size of my thigh, and I'm no waif. I may not have inherited the Bennet boobs like my sisters, but I definitely got the Bennet legs. Thigh gaps don't exist around these parts.

He's dressed in what I can only describe as a kilt. Although it looks more like the skirts pharaohs wear in Egyptian hieroglyphics. Everything else is bare and buff. Burly muscles twist beneath skin so silver that it almost looks painted on. Even this isn't so strange when I've been shacking up with Bati, whose skin is a midnight blue. It's the bit happening around his chest that throws me off.

He has a plume. Layers of sleek, bright yellow feathers fan out over his pecs and across his shoulders. It's almost like he has a set of wings, but instead of them being on his back, they're on his front. They're delicate and beautiful against his silver skin. Everything about him is a contradiction. Even when he held me to stop me from jumping in the water, his grip was gentle. His voice was soothing. "Be easy, little one," he'd said. He's kind of a scary looking dude, but he moves about his small camping area with fluid, surprisingly graceful movements.

"He is Somii," Bati returns as he pulls apart one of two steaming bags of veggies he heated on the cooking pad. The word sounds like *sum-eye*. And like that plume of feathers on his chest, it's delicate for such a brutal looking species.

I'm distracted by the smell of food and look down into the bag that Bati has arranged in the middle of our little circle. The veggies inside are yellow and almost look like boiled potatoes smothered in butter sauce. Before waiting for my instruction, KJ sticks his fork into the bag and lifts a chunk to his mouth.

"Careful, *dahni*. It is hot," Bati warns before holding out a piece on a fork for me. I lean forward and close my mouth around it. Immediately, my eyes widen.

"This tastes like cheese eggs!" I moan around my mouthful. The texture is a little chunkier than eggs, but it definitely has that same cheesy, buttery taste. I pick up my fork and dip into the bag for another chunk then hold it out to Bati. Holding my gaze, he leans forward and takes the food. His large, bright teeth flash briefly.

"This is *bom*," he says, chewing slowly. "I remember on Earth your family prepared bird eggs for breakfast. My mother suggested this preparation for a similar taste."

"It's yummy!" KJ does a little dance as he forks another chunk into his mouth. Bati's eyebrow shoots up and his mouth hitches to the side as he gives my son the Lyqa version of side-eye.

"That is interesting, *dahni*, because you previously said it tastes like kaka."

I sputter and choke on my mouthful, my eyes shooting over to KJ, who at least has the decency to look somewhat ashamed. This kid, man.

"KJ, what did I tell you about calling food kaka? It's not nice."

Bati laughs. "It is okay, Tiani. I do not know what kaka means, anyway."

"Trust me, you don't want to know," I return and shake my head in a way that lets him know it isn't good. "Either way, he knows better. Don't you, K?" I shoot KJ a look, and he looks quickly away, which is good because I'm having a hard time keeping a straight face.

We eat in silence for a moment before the Somii guy's movements at the other end of the platform draw my attention once again.

He's pitching a tent. Unlike Bati's high-tech, sound proof dome, this guy has a straight up old fashioned, stick beneath a blanket tent. He's currently arranging several large rocks along the base to hold down the sides.

"Is he here on *ta'ani ma*thingie, too?"

"He is on a different kind of quest," Bati replies. I wait for him to elaborate, and when he doesn't, I pick back up my fork and continue to eat.

We finish the bag, and I'm stuffed. Lyqa food must be denser than Earth veggies because I find I eat less but get full quicker. I point to the unopened bag.

"It's going to go to waste."

"It will not." Bati looks in the direction of the Somii guy. A second later, the guy turns from his tent and strolls over to us. He settles his large form into the space between Bati and KJ, and like the little beast that he is, KJ scoots closer, peering up at him with shameless interest.

"What's your name?"

I groan inside and press a hand to my forehead. "K, honey —"

"It is acceptable for your youngling to ask me questions," the man declares in his even, monotone voice. I stare back at him, a little unsettled. There is something strange about his face. Everything is angular but also flat. His jaw is chiseled, but so much so that each angle is sharp and pointy. Bright orange eyes peek from just below lids that are so smooth they almost look two dimensional. He looks sleepy, or like he smoked the fattest J there ever was. The bridge of his nose is a flat plane that narrows down before fanning out into two slightly flared nostrils. He's kind of surreal to look at. It doesn't help that he only has one expression.

He looks down at KJ. A quiet moment passes then KJ's eyes widen and his mouth forms into a little 'o'.

"Mommy, he said something in my ears!" he gasps, turning his stunned expression on me.

I frown, laughing a bit, and turned to Bati.

"What does he mean?"

"Somii are telepaths," Bati states simply. I blink and blink again. I continue to stare at him, but inside my head, I'm imagining the largest atomic mushroom cloud ever. Mind.

Blown.

"Why does my method of communication inspire thoughts of destruction?"

My head swivels back to the guy. His expressionless eyes are trained on me.

"Oh my god, can you see inside of my fucking head?"

"Mommy…"

"I know, baby. I'm sorry."

"But can you see inside of my freaking head?"

"I can."

I gasp, my hands coming up to cover my mouth. My eyes are as wide as KJ's.

I get what was so weird about his face now. When he talks, he doesn't move his mouth.

BATI

"Mind, fucking, blown."

Tiani mumbles this under her breath, yet again. I do not understand what this expression means, but I agree that it sounds violent. Our guest is gracious. While he is more comfortable speaking telepathically, he shares his responses to Tiani with me.

"I am Soluanitiat'ti Somiiti'un, but you may call me Sol if it is more comfortable."

My *lehti* stares with her mouth agape for a very long moment. When she finally speaks, her voice is an awed whisper.

"Tiani, but you can call me Tee."

Sol inclines his head politely. "It is a pleasure to meet you, Tee. I am glad you did not harm yourself attempting to traverse the seas earlier."

Tiani's head hinges in my direction. Her eyes are wide as they fix on me.

"Dude, this is so fucking weird," she whispers. I halt the urge to smile. It is clear that my *lehti* does not fully grasp how Somii communication works.

"He can still hear you, Tiani," I inform her, and her face brightens the slightest bit before she turns back to Sol.

"I am so sorry, but I'm from Earth, and all of us talk with our mouths. We only see this kind of shit in movies."

Her eyes flicker down to KJ, but he isn't paying attention. All of his focus is on Sol. Periodically, he laughs. Tiani leans into me, keeping her eyes on the pair.

"Uh, is he having a side conversation with our kid?" She speaks out of the side of her mouth, her face alight with excitement.

My heart thumps. She continues to watch KJ laugh up at Sol, unaware of how her words have impacted me. *Our kid.* Until this moment, I have only hoped that one day Tiani would regard us as a family. That she would speak of us as one and KJ as our own. My first heart fills with an indescribable joy. It blossoms throughout my chest, and I reach out for her, pulling her into my lap, and cradling her against me.

I do not respond for I do not wish to spoil the moment. Tiani lets me hold her for a while and then she leans her head back, looking up at me in concern.

"You okay?" Her nose is scrunched in the middle.

"I am perfect, my *lehti*."

Her bewilderment deepens but she angles her face up and presses her mouth to mine. Her hand comes up to cup my jaw, and I tilt my head, deepening the kiss.

"What is this thing you do with your mouths?"

Tiani yelps and jerks away. For a moment, I am filled with annoyance that the Somii has interrupted me tasting my *lehti,* but then I realize that we are not alone. I will have Tiani to myself tonight. Until then, her lush, soft lips against mine will have to suffice.

"It is kissing." I ease away from Tiani but keep her on my lap. This is partly because I like her against me but also because my cock is impossibly hard. When she shifts, pushing her plump bottom against me, I groan, and she chuckles softly.

"What is this kissing?"

The Somii stares back and forth between us, his expression stuck in the same placid form. Somii as a species have limited emotional expression. Where Lyqa, as a kind, are feelers, always in tune to the emotions and moods of others, Somii can sense the feelings of others, but can only experience pain. And even then, it is only the pain of others they can experience when they witness it. This has led to the Somii being an exceptionally peaceful society, but has also limited their ability to socialize with other societies that are less peaceful. I was quite surprised when I awoke to find a Somii male setting up camp on the sea willow with us. They are not often seen off of their home planet.

Tiani clears her throat. "Uh, I guess it's like a kind of way of showing affection. A way of showing love or an attraction to another person."

My heart stutters when she says the word "love." The Somii studies me with interest; although, he is not very expressive. His scent is flat, but there is the tiniest hint of curiosity beneath it.

"You are paired? Is this why you kiss?"

That tinge of embarrassment colors Tiani's scent again. The tips of her ears brighten beneath her brown skin, and she shifts again in my lap.

"Uh, we are in a thing. I mean, I guess we're kind of dating."

Sol tilts his head. "Is dating coupling? Is that why you are thinking of him *fukhing* you?" He pronounces the English word with a heavy accent.

"Oh, god." Tiani covers her ears and starts to shake her head back and forth. "No, no. I can't. Make him stop." Her embarrassment is sharp.

"Please prevent yourself from viewing her thoughts, friend. It makes her uncomfortable."

Immediately, a silence descends that I had not noticed was missing. It is as if a door has been closed. Tiani, too, blinks and looks up at me.

"That was too weird," she whispers and turns her face into my chest. I take a deep breath and close my eyes. At once, I wish I had Sol's ability. I would know what he saw in her mind just now.

"Do not struggle against me, *lehti*. You must relax."

Tiani is upright in the water. I brace my hand beneath her legs and apply pressure up with the hand splayed below her back. We have been in the water for nearly an hour, and I am beginning to believe my *lehti* is hopeless.

"Okay, okay. I'm relaxed." Tiani exhales a lungful of air, and I roll my eyes.

"*Lehti*, you will not float if you are not buoyant. You become buoyant by having air in your lungs."

"Well, how am I supposed to relax if I'm holding my breath?" Tiani huffs out in frustration. She tenses. It is not good for her to speak. She cannot focus.

"Take shadow breaths, mommy!"

"Shallow, baby."

"Take shallow breaths, mommy!"

KJ paddles by us in the water. His little legs kick up sprays of water that make Tiani flinch.

"KJ, practice your cupcake hands over there." I tilt my head at an empty space a few feet away.

"Not too far!"

Tiani's shout is followed by an attempt to lift her head, which causes her bottom to drop. She wraps her arms around my neck. Her legs wrap around my waist and tighten, bringing her core against me. I feel her heat immediately. Even in the warm water, it flares through my body. Help me.

I cup her bottom and hold her still. She's breathing hard from her efforts, and I can't help but shake my head. My poor, non-amphibious *lehti*. She is definitely nothing like a fish.

"I'm never going to get this," she mutters, and I dislike the defeat I smell on her.

"You will get it, *lehti*. But you must relax."

"Do you know how hard it is to relax with you right here?" She presses her face into my shoulder and groans. "When you said you were going to teach me to swim, I thought you meant we were going to play around. You know, have a little hanky panky in the water. I didn't think you meant to seriously teach me to swim. I obviously suck at it."

"It is simple once you get it, Tiani. It will happen. You do not suck."

Abruptly, her scent turns mischievous, and she lifts her head to peer at me. "You know what I just realized?" she murmurs and leans in to kiss me. I return the slight pressure of her lips before answering.

"What have you noticed, my *lehti*?"

"I've never given you head. We should remedy that. Like right now."

Head? Is this some kind of human social exchange? Her scent grows decidedly sneaky and it piques my interest.

"I do not know what this means, 'to give head.' You must explain it to me," I reply honestly.

Her mouth curves up and she leans over my shoulder. Her lips brush over the sensitive flesh of my ear and I falter in the water. Our bodies dip slightly.

"It means to suck your dick."

My cock flares to life, rising rapidly behind my thin shorts. The image her words conjure sends a thrill through my body that makes it impossible for me to tread water with any grace. I maneuver us the few feet to the platform's ledge and take hold. KJ holds on to the platform nearby.

"K, it is time to leave of the water, *dahni*. Ask Sol to help you."

"Okay!"

It's quiet, and a moment later, the platform shakes with the Somii's heavy footfalls. KJ laughs and then I hear the sound of dripping water as he's pulled from the sea.

"We are in need of privacy, friend. Could you see to our son?"

"Of course. I will ensure he stays away from this side of the ledge."

"He has those Lyqa blocks. Sit him down to play, and he'll be fine."

My eyes widen on Tiani's face as her voice rings out in my head. I did not realize Sol was sharing.

Sol gives a soft grunt of confirmation before the silence of his telepathic disconnect descends over us once more. I turn my attention back to Tiani. Her scent is playful and light.

"You seek to tempt me with this 'head' to get out of the water, but I must insist you complete your lesson."

Her legs are still wrapped tightly around me. I move my hand from her bottom and slip it between us, sliding it down her belly and against the heat of her pussy.

"Bati!" Her voice is a surprised gasp. She is wearing her undergarments. Something called a bra and panties. I push aside the thin, triangle of fabric and my hands immediately come in contact with her slick folds. Even in water, I can tell the difference in her arousal. It is silky, and my long fingers glide over her flesh with ease.

"Mm, oh!" she moans as I continue to explore her.

"Your first lesson, my *lehti,* is you must relax to float properly, and in order to relax, you must be quiet. Can you be quiet?"

The dark pools of her eyes stare into mine. I remove my hand from between her legs and reach into my shorts, freeing my cock. It springs up hard and long between us.

"God, you're so huge. I don't know how you get that in me."

The way she stares at my cock, with a mixture of awe and excitement, makes the tip leak a thick bead of semen.

"You were made for me, my *lehti*. Your pussy was fashioned to take me." As I speak, I lift her with my free hand until she hovers above the tip just outside of the water. "Guide me, Tiani. Put my cock inside of you."

She releases an arm from my neck and reaches between us to grip me. Her hips flex forward and her hot center closes over me.

"*Hu'l!*" It is too good. The weightlessness of the water only serves to heighten the sensation of pushing through her tight passage. I hold her around the back, pressing our bodies together until I'm seated deep inside of her.

"Oh, my god, Bati. I still can't believe you curse."

Her voice is tinged with amusement. I press firmly on her back, driving even further inside of her, and she gasps.

"Quiet, remember," I whisper against her lips. Our movements are somewhat awkward in the water. "I must keep us above water. When I kick my legs, you press against me, yes?"

I'm barely holding on. The need to release became nearly unbearable the moment I entered her. I will not last long, but I will not go until she joins me.

Tiani nods her head and folds her lips in. Our hearts keep a furious beat between us. The anticipation coloring her scent reflects my own.

I bring my knees up with my feet together before fanning them out. The movement propels me up out of the water. At the same moment, I flex my hips to meet Tiani's downward motion. My cock hammers up into her pussy.

"Ah!"

We both still following her exclamation. The water laps loudly around us.

"Quiet, my *lehti.*"

"I'm sorry, it just feels so good."

Her words are a desperate moan that send my brain into a frenzy. I kick my legs again, pulling her down as I propel out of the water, and again my cock drives deep, pressing solidly through her passage.

"Mm!"

The sound is muffled behind her lips. I keep this pace, treading water, each thrust lodging me deeper inside of her and bringing me closer and closer to my end. Tiani's eyes are shut tightly as she takes the drive of my hips propelling up from the water. The only sound she makes is those little muffled moans. Her body is tense. She's close but needs something more.

"Pull down your top," I whisper.

Her eyes open, and a fresh gush of silky wetness surrounds me on my next plunge upward. She yanks at the scrap of material covering her breasts. The moment they're bared to me, I lower my head and latch onto one of her nipples, drawing hard on the tight bud.

"Ah, Bati, please."

I come wetly off of her. She pleads up at me with a pained expression.

"I know, my love. My *lehti*. I will give you what you need."

I turn us so that her back rests against the side of the sea willow. I bring my legs up and brace them on the underside, catching a foothold for leverage.

I ease slowly out of her before hinging my hips forward, driving deep and hitting her core.

"Bati!"

I do it again, each time increasing the pace until my entire body burns with the effort of working her pussy and keeping up afloat. My release is an ache in my balls, but I hold it at bay until she starts to shake. Little gasps escape her mouth and I drive harder and faster until she moans low and long, her orgasm finally rippling through her. Only then do I press deep and let go, filling her with a flood of semen.

I release my foothold and let the water carry me from her body. Tiani falls limply against me, her arms loose about my shoulders. I push off from the platform and ease her away. Her body stays pliant as I lift her beneath the legs and lower her onto her back.

Her eyes are closed. Her breath sounds out in little huffs. I hold her steady for a moment and then release her. She bobs gently, her body level above the water.

"Tiani."

"Hm?" Her acknowledgment is a serene murmur in her throat.

"You're floating."

Chapter 13

TIANI

"Mommy, are you going to float all day?"

I blink my eyes open. I've only been here for about five minutes, but I enjoyed the bit of Zen time. KJ's round little face peers down at me from the platform.

"Bati!" I call out, trying not to move too much. I've got the float down, but anything else and I'm a flailing mess.

"I am here." He's right next to me. I start, my body immediately collapsing. I take a breath, preparing to go under, but Bati's large hands slide beneath me, keeping me afloat. "I think you have practiced enough. Low tide is approaching again. We should be able to continue our *ta'ani* by mid-day."

He lets my lower body drop into the water. I cross my arms around his shoulders and turn into him, wrapping my legs around his waist. His bright blue eyes smile down at me.

"Did I do well?"

The waves lap slowly against our joined bodies. The rolling motion pushes us together, and I gasp when the hard ridge of his dick nudges against me.

"You did perfectly, my *lehti*." He leans in to press a soft kiss to my lips. "I will teach you to tread water next, but not today."

I don't even try to stop my grateful sigh. "Thank god. I don't think I can do much more."

"What you have done today is enough. At least for swimming." The blue of his eyes twinkles brightly, and I go warm all over.

"Mm, that's right. I still owe you some head." He's still nibbling at my mouth and I catch his full bottom lip and suck it gently. He groans.

"Not owed, but if you are feeling generous later, I will not reject your offer of affection."

This is one of the things I love about Bati. He's so respectful, and it doesn't put a damper on us being hot for each other. It makes me want to give him more, knowing he doesn't expect it.

"I think I'll be feeling very generous later," I murmur against his lips.

"And I shall be very grateful."

"Tiani, please!"

"Shh. They're going to hear us."

I swirl my tongue around the head of Bati's dick again, and he groans even louder before falling back onto the floor of the tent. He tastes sweet. Not like sugar, but the way fresh, clean water tastes sweet. His skin is smooth and warm. I can't stop myself from lapping at the tight flesh over and over.

"The—ah—the tent is discreet, but, Tee, please. It is too much."

He hasn't seen anything, yet. I run my tongue slowly from the base of his dick all the way to the tip.

"Hu'l." The curse is a soft hiss. I love it when he says that. For some reason, I didn't think Lyqas had things like curse words, but every time he says that word, *hool*, my translator

definitely murmurs *shit* into my head.

When I get to the tip of his dick, I close my mouth over it and suck hard. Bati groans. His voice is harsh. Satisfaction rushes through me.

I keep forgetting he was a big ol' virgin before we met. I love that I get to wow him with all the fun stuff about sex. And right now, he is definitely wowed.

"Tiani, I will not last."

I don't want him to. I've obviously given head before, but the way Bati responds has me feeling all kinds of powerful. I lower my head, easing him into my mouth and down my throat, moving my tongue along the way.

"*Lehti*!" the growl that erupts from his throat makes me jump, but a second later, his dick starts to jerk in my mouth and a squirt of cum hits my throat. I swallow around it and keep swallowing as he cums. When I can't take anymore, I pull him out of my mouth and lean over him, jerking the rest off on my tits.

"I would say that I enjoyed that immeasurably," he sighs out once his body settles. "I would also express my gratitude to you for being such a generous lover."

"You don't have to thank me, Bati. It's my pleasure."

He lifts up lightning fast and flips us over, coming between my legs and sliding into me in one smooth stroke.

"Mm." I will never get enough of having him inside of me, of being stretched. The delicious ache.

"You feel so good," I murmur. The feeling is so intense that the moment he starts to move, my orgasm pulses through me.

"It is a two-mile-long journey from here to the west forests. I will carry KJ when he tires. Are you able to walk that distance?"

"I think so."

Bati's re-packing our bags. I take the one he holds out to

me and sling it onto my back. KJ stands a few feet away with his little pack hitched over his shoulders. He's holding his back straight and looking very seriously. He's not playing about this *ta'ani*thing. He wants to win, even though I am pretty sure there is absolutely no prize at the end. He taps his foot impatiently as he waits for us to leave.

"Aww, we're gonna be late," he whines when Bati rechecks his bag before swinging it around his back. He secures the straps and turns an admonishing glance on KJ.

"*Ta'ani maul* is nothing if not an exercise in patience, my *dahni*. The items we are searching for require a keen eye and an unhurried mind. Do you think you are able to display these characteristics? We will not be successful otherwise."

Bati's mouth quirks up a tiny bit, and his eyes glance over to me, quickly. He's so full of shit. He's already told me the things on the list are almost all laying around our campsite platform. He's just playing it up for the kid.

KJ's little body snaps to attention. He pulls his shoulders back again, assuming his previous pose of seriousness.

"Yup. I can do it. I can be sussessful."

Bati confirms with a short jerk of his head and pulls out the thin slip of plastic-like material that has the list.

"You were very successful in retrieving the *wuor'gi*, but the next item is slightly more difficult to find." He kneels down so that he's on level with KJ and holds the list out for him to see. "This is *aiguu*. It is a rare succulent that only grows deep in the west forests." KJ peers closely at the list. It's in Lyqa. The kid can't even read in English yet, but his eyes float over the list with interest.

"What's it look like?"

"It is a short bulbous red plant, marked with long, purple spikes. This can make extraction precarious, but if one is careful, it can be done."

"Oh." KJ does his knowing little nod again, and I have to

smother a laugh.

I look down at the ground. A few feet away, near the edge of the platform, is a small shrub. Red globes, no bigger than a strawberry, sprout from the mossy base. Each globe has three or four pointy pistils sticking from the middle. The light breeze bends them easily.

"They are not very dangerous. I promise," Bati murmurs as he comes to stand beside me. He's left KJ with the list, probably so he doesn't notice the *aiguu* sitting a few feet away.

"I know." I turn to face him. My heart thumps heavily. Something really close to love rushes through me as I look up into his warm, blue eyes. "You're so sweet. I love how you are with him. Thank you."

"You do not have to thank me, Tiani. I would have this trip be fun for him. And for you." He steps around me and swats my ass before strolling off to speak with Sol who's standing a few feet away.

Sol is cool. A few times, I've caught him watching me and Bati. Particularly when we're kissing or being otherwise affectionate. Bati said his people aren't really the lovey-dovey types. The single expression he's had since he showed up makes this pretty obvious.

"Is Bati my dad?"

My head tilts slowly down to where KJ looks up at me with innocent curiosity. I press my eyes closed for a long moment before opening them again. My heart beats fast. KJ stares up at me, waiting patiently for my answer.

"What?" Maybe he'll forget the question.

"Is Bati my dad," he asks again like it's the most obvious question in the world. "He acts like my dad, I think. He tells me stuff. He takes me places. He gives me candy, and you kiss him all the time. So, he's my dad, right?"

My son's simple assessment of what constitutes

parenthood makes me pissed for a moment that his actual father found parenting too complicated for his life. A wave of anxiety washes over me as I open my mouth to reply.

"K, you know Grammy Spence. That's your father's mother, remember? You met Bati's mommy before. They aren't the same person, so he can't be your dad."

KJ's face falls. His shoulders droop forward, and he kicks at a small rock at his foot. "Oh."

My heart breaks a little. He and Bati are so good together and have gotten so close, but I don't want to lie to him. Even as my attachment to Bati grows, and the idea that we are bound to each other in some fateful way takes root in my mind, I can't just lead my son to believe something that may not work out in the end. I've been careful about doing this until now, and I don't think it's a good idea to change up the script just because I got googly-eyes for Bati. My throat tightens when KJ sighs in disappointment.

"May I say something to him? I will not contradict what you have told him."

I turn to find Bati standing just behind me. Of course, he heard. A slight smile curves his mouth, but it's sad. He kneels down in front of KJ and chucks him beneath the chin.

"KJ, you are a very beautiful, smart, magical child. From the moment I saw you, I knew this to be true. I am not your father, biologically, but here," he presses his hand over his first heart, "I love you as if you are mine. I love you, and I love your mother. I will always care for you and help you. It does not matter where you are. You are my *dahni,* and I am your *ahpa*. Do you understand?"

I cover my mouth because I'm very close to crying. When KJ propels himself forward and hugs Bati around the neck, my eyes start to sting.

Bati holds KJ close, hugging him tightly and rocking slightly back and forth.

"Are you going to go away? When I have to go home?"

Bati's eyes rise to meet mine. They're glassy and bright. The blue sparkles intensely.

"I will never leave, my *dahni*. Not ever."

Our gazes are locked. His promise reaches all the way to my spirit, and the perfectly synchronized thump of Bati's heart over mine, seals it as truth.

BATI

"Well that got intense, huh?"

Tiani smells nervous. She has smelled this way since our moment at the campsite. I did not expect KJ's questioning of his mother. I also did not expect the surge of longing I caught on Tiani's scent when she responded. Her longing shifted to affection after I'd made my promise. I can only hope what that affection means.

She moves slowly beside me. The hem of her skirt keeps snagging on the rough stalks of sea sponge that poke up from the mud. Her thin Qitoni sandals suck through the sludge, and I feel another moment of guilt at having had such an impractical dress made for her.

"I apologize, *lehti*. It is my fault you are having such a hard time."

She looks up from where she's trying her best to tie the bottom of her skirt into a knot.

"I mean, it's not your fault Qitoni fashion sucks." She tries again to pull the fabric taut on itself, but it unravels every time. Sighing, she gives up and straightens. I can feel my face pulsing brightly. "What?"

"This is not the only choice of Qitoni fashion. There were other more practical choices. Pants," I admit. "This particular style was simply more—revealing."

She stares at me for a moment and then erupts into

laughter.

"Are you serious? Dude, you had an entire dress made just so you could check out my boobs?"

"It did not ask for the design to be modified for this purpose, but I was not unaware that this would be the subsequent result."

She quirks an eyebrow and regards me with amusement.

"You realize you probably would have seen them anyway, right? I mean, we were going away together."

I can't stop my frown. Has she learned nothing of me? "I would not assume such a thing."

"Dude, you brought a shared tent," she shoots back, and her mouth twists up to the side.

I blush again. "I hoped, but had nothing occurred between us, I would have been content to merely be in your presence."

"There's the *argoo*!"

KJ puts a halt to our conversation. We both turn to the spot where his tiny finger stabs through the air. Nestled at the base of a cluster of seaweed trees is a fully developed *aiguu*. It has the same round bulbs as the smaller one on the platform, but each one is nearly the size of my entire body. Three-foot-tall purple pistils shoot up into sharp points. The edges drip with the toxic sap it is known for.

"Holy cow, that's the same as the one at the camp?" Tiani's voice is shocked as she follows me through the thick mud until we get close.

"The one at the willow was a fledgling. They grow best in damp conditions," I return. I stop several feet away. This task is simple enough, but for humans, unused to traversing such wilderness, it poses a greater threat than I previously thought. I will have to be extra diligent.

From my shoulders, KJ's awed gasp sounds out. "Wow! It's a giant!"

"How the heck are we supposed to get that back with us?

Do we just take a piece?"

I chuckle and lift my wrist, tapping my citizenship band. "Of course not, *lehti*. This plant is quite toxic when fully developed. We will take a picture." The flash on the side of my band brightens briefly before a holographic image of the plant fans from the top. "See?"

I angle my wrist up for them.

"So that's it. We just take a photo and bring it back? Does someone check it or something?"

"We can submit our results to the regulators of the game for recording. Many have made it a life's mission to complete all levels of *ta'ani*. We are just doing the basic version of this particular quest."

Tiani regards the sharp blades of the *aiguu* again. "What's the hardest one?"

"To procure a seed from the middle of the pod without damage to the plant."

"Where are the seeds?" She peers closely at the blades, taking a small step forward.

"The seeds are protected by the pistils at the center. They only open at a particular time of year, and only when the plant is fully submerged." I catch the back of her top, stopping her inspection just as she gets too close for my comfort. She looks back at me with shock.

"You mean, you have to find the seeds in that dark ass water with these friggin Freddy Krueger knives sticking all over the place?"

I do not know who or what Freddy Krueger is, but I nod.

"Can you guys see through the water?"

I shake my head. Lyqa senses are good, but not supernatural. "As I said before, these can be quite elaborate."

She looks impressed. "Damn. I mean, that's kind of badass, but damn. I thought you said Lyqas don't do unnecessarily dangerous situations?"

I shrug. "To some, challenging one's physical limits is necessary. We are given this form. It is not wrong to use it."

She rolls her eyes and shakes her head. "That is some whypipo shit, if I ever heard it. Let me find out."

I do not know what she refers to, but her scent is teasing so I assume her response is good natured.

"Come, if we hurry, we can gather the remaining items and be back to the camp site before high tide."

I move around the *aiguu,* making sure to keep a wide berth. Though generally harmless if avoided, if one were to get *aiguu* toxin on their skin, it would be unfortunate.

The further we move into the forest, the more dense the terrain gets. The sun is high in sky. I check my wristband for signs of danger. I also follow the progress of the shadows in the forest. We only have a few more hours before high tide returns.

"Stay close to me, *lehti.*"

"Oh, trust me, I'm two steps behind you."

"Stay a single step behind me."

Tiani grips the back of my shirt and the small contact warms me. I lift KJ from my shoulders and hold him in front of me. The branches overhead are beginning to hang low.

"What's next?" He pulls the list from his pocket and holds it up. I spare the list the smallest glance before I train my eyes on the forest ahead of me. Qitoni is a generally safe planet. It's aquatic nature and long low tides mean that not many large predators preside on land. But it also means that most of the danger comes from plant life. I will have to be mindful of what we touch.

"Next, we must find the *gaurgii,* a small burrowing fish that lives in the mud at the base of living sea willows."

"Goggie," KJ repeats. Unlike my *sa'aih* Amina, my *lehti*'s Lyqa pronunciation is terrible. My *dahni*'s is not much better, but he is a child, and it makes him no less endearing. Possibly more so.

"Yes, my *dahni*, goggie," I confirm.

"Where can we find it?" Tiani's asks behind me.

"It resides at the base of the red sea willow."

"Is that like the one we were camped on, but red?"

"And smaller. Our campsite is a giant sea willow. However, it is no longer living and has been petrified. The sea willow we are looking for will be alive."

"Hm." I glance back. Tiani's looking around, trying to spot the tree.

We move past the dense portion of the forest, and the foliage begins to thin again. The branches overhead rise a bit higher and I move KJ back to my shoulders.

"Keep a keen eye out for the *gaurgii*, KJ."

"I'm looking!"

My Lyqa senses are also on alert. Off to the side, a small shelled creature, which is known for catching and dissolving insects and other small fish, waits with its mouth opened wide. At the center, a bright flowerlike tongue serves to trick unsuspecting pollinators.

A second later, something slithers across my foot. I look down. A large sea snake moves through the wet mud. While not particularly dangerous, I imagine if Tiani were to notice it, she would not be pleased. I have not forgotten how she and her sister reacted to the bug that flew into our home on Lyqa. I don't mention it. Instead, I draw her attention to the various plant life around us.

I point to a small patch of thin, blue reeds winding up the side of an algae plant. "Those vines connect to the host planet. They function very similarly to the nerves in other species."

"It can feel? The planet?" Her voice sounds awed.

"It can. Although, it is does not react to stimuli as sensitively as you or I might."

"So, if I pinch it, it won't like squeal?" her tinkling laughter washes over me, and I reach back to pull her beside me, joining our hands. I want to see her.

She falls in line beside me. Her beautiful, full mouth is pulled into a wide smile. Her eyes, although they are as dark as night, are warm and gentle.

"You are beautiful, my *lehti*." I can't resist saying it. I will never tire of seeing her, feeling her, loving her.

"You're not too bad, yourself, Lyqa dude." She laughs again, and I have to force my eyes back on the forest because I should be looking out for danger, but all I want to do is taste her.

Up ahead, in a small clearing, the bright red branches of a sea willow come into view. They are the easiest plants to spot in the forest. I knew it would not be long before we came upon one.

"Isn't that—" I squeeze our joined hands, silencing Tiani. When she frowns up at me, I shake my head, indicating she should wait.

"The goggie!" KJ shouts out a second later, and I rise my eyebrows. Tiani brings our hands up to kiss the back of mine.

"You're so flipping sweet."

My skin tingles where her lips touched me.

"Yes, KJ, that is the sea willow where we will find the *gaurgii*." I lower him to the ground when we get to the willow. He steps forward, staring closely at the trunk.

"Is it safe to touch?"

I turn to Tiani. She's worriedly watching KJ.

"It is fine. They are harmless. Touch it."

They both reach out to push their fingertips against the soft, squishy bark. Thick, black water oozes out. "Yuck!"

They both exclaim it at the same time, and I chuckle.

"It is just water."

Tiani and KJ share a similar comical look of disgust.

"So how do we find this *ta'ani*thing?" she asks.

KJ looks up eagerly, and I kneel down beside him and point to a small mound of mud at the base of the tree. "The *gaurgii* lives in there. All we must do it make it come out so we can capture a picture."

"How do we make it come out?" The excitement rolling off of him is full of the wonder of childhood. It makes me glad that I brought them here.

"We must call it, *dahni.*"

KJ drops to the ground, planting his hands on either side of the mound and lowering his face over it. "Come out, goggie! Come out!"

I don't fight my smile. "No, *dahni,* we must call him in a special way. *Gaurgii* only come out during low tide to catch their favorite food. It is a small insect that emits a medium pitched song, but one must replicate the song perfectly to call it."

KJ jabs his finger at his mother. "Let mommy do it. She can sing really good."

Chapter 14

TIANI

"You are a singer?" Bati looks questioningly up at me from where he's kneeling next to KJ.

"Uh, no. I can kind of carry a tune, but I am definitely *not* a singer."

He stands and waves a hand at the mound. "Carry the tune."

"No, I'm not singing."

"Mommy, pleeeease! We need the goggie to come out!"

I can't help but laugh at how KJ pronounces the name of the fish. The way he says it, I know he isn't thinking of a fish at all. He's probably imagining some cross between a puppy and a tadpole.

"Ugh, fine! What is it supposed to sound like?"

I clear my throat in preparation and feel stupid. If I was on Earth, my friends would be rolling their eyes at the extraness of it.

Bati's mouth quirk's up, and I know he's about to make me embarrass myself.

"How about you sing a song with a good range of notes, and I will stop you when you get to the right one?"

"If you know what it's supposed to sound like, why don't you call it?" I ask, arching an eyebrow.

"I would rather hear you, my *lehti*."

He waits. KJ, too, looks expectantly up at me.

"God, I can't believe I'm doing this," I mumble before kneeling in the mud next to the mound. "La, la, la, la la," I sound out, going along the scale, except I sing it very quickly and without much effort. When I look at Bati, his eyes are narrowed on me.

"I think you can do better than that. Now, again, and so that I may hear you properly. Or else, I will not be able to discern the note."

I roll my eyes and take a deep breath. This is mortifying, but I may as well get it over with.

"Laaa...laaa...laaa...laaa...laaa," I sound again. This time slower and louder.

When I stop, Bati has something of wonder on his face. "You are truly a beautiful woman. Your voice is lovely." He leans in to press a smacking kiss on my mouth before I even realize it. "Now, I believe the second note is correct. You must be loud if the *gaurgii* is to hear you, and you must get close."

"Do I just make the same sound I did?" I ask as I put my hands on either side of the mound and lean in like KJ did.

"It may be more convincing as the bug if you hum it." His smile is sly. I know he's getting a kick out of this. I roll my eyes again and lean down close to the mound.

"Mmmmmmmmmm," I hold the note as long as I can. Suddenly, the mound shifts, and I jump back.

"Okay, *dahni*, the *gaurgii* will emerge. When it does, use your band like I showed you to capture it."

KJ's face sets in determination and he raises his arm, angling it at the mound. The middle of the mud sinks in, and a second later two short green antennae rise from the hole that's revealed. The long, slimy body of what looks almost like a slug with the head of a catfish rises up from the mound. It's not that big. Maybe only the size of my hand.

"Capture it before it retreats," Bati urges, and KJ taps his band causing the screen to flash up. He presses into the projection, and his camera flashes in the same way Bati's did when he took a picture of the *aiguu*. As soon as the light blinks, the *gaurgii* drops back into the hole with a wet sucking sound.

"I got it!" KJ raises his arm up triumphantly.

"You did very well, *dahni*," Bati returns and then surprises me by raising his hand up flat in front of KJ. KJ lifts his own hand and slaps their palms together.

"Hi five!" They say together, and my heart thumps.

An hour later of us wandering through the forest, and we stand at the edge of another clearing. Along the way, Bati has been showing us the different plants and sea creatures, including a flat eel that ran across my feet and nearly scared me to death. He has also been showing me the parts of the forest that are extensions of the host planet, so I remember what he told me before when I see the cluster of blue vines. I still can't believe the thing we're on is alive. I keep expecting to see a mouth or a limb or something crazy even though Bati has done a good job of keeping us distracted.

"Do you remember what those are, *dahni*?" Bati points to a large, tangled cluster. The vines wind stiffly up into the air, so they look almost like a bunch of skinny twigs.

KJ's head bobbles. "Yup. Nerds."

"Nerves, baby. With a v, like in violin."

"Nerbbbbsuh," KJ tries again.

Bati turns his face in my direction so KJ can't see, and his mouth breaks into a wide, soundless laugh. I blink. Bati's so serious, and this is so silly that I have to cover my own mouth to keep from cracking up. He shakes his head and twists his mouth until his expression is stoic again.

"Yes, my *dahni*. These are nerves. They connect to the host planet. They help it feel."

"If I touch them, he can feel it?" KJ's eyes are wide.

"I believe so," Bati returns.

"What does it feel like?"

Bati twists his mouth up to the side as if he's considering the question. "Hm, I do not know. Perhaps like this!" His free hand attacks KJ at his sides, and my son squeals and giggles under Bati's tickling fingers.

They're so good together. So natural. To anyone looking on, there would be no question they are father and son, aside from the alien thing. That tightening happens in my throat again, but it's not sadness like it was before. It's happiness and acceptance.

"Why are you crying, Tiani? You do not smell sad."

I blink up. Bati and KJ wear nearly identical expressions of confusion, and it's just too much. I throw myself against Bati's side, wrapping my arms around his waist, and press my face against the hard panel of his abs.

"I love you, Bati. I love you so much."

He stiffens, but I keep squeezing. I want to crawl inside of him. I just want to be as close as I can. It's so stupid that I haven't been telling him I love him since the day I met him, because I'm pretty sure I have.

"Tiani?"

I lift my face. He's looking down at me, and he still looks confused. His brows, which I'm just noticing are the same red color as his curly hair, are bunched low over his eyes. He looks young this close up. I'll have to ask him how old his is one of these days.

"Call me *lehti*. I like it." I try for a smile, but it's nervous and wobbly.

The muscles in his throat jerk beneath his smooth midnight

skin.

"Lehti."

His bright blue eyes search my face. He's looking at me like he doesn't believe what I've said, so I make sure there's no question.

"I love you, Bati. I love your sweet, sexy, beautiful, awesome guts, dude. And if you'll let us, I want to stay with you forever."

He stares at me for a long time then blinks.

"*Dahni,* I must put you down for a moment. Is that okay?"

"Yup!" Bati sets KJ on his feet and the kid immediately pulls a block from somewhere on his person and busies himself.

Bati straightens and turns back to me. I get all fidgety as he steps close. The heat from his body radiates between us. I can hear his heart. It's thumping hard. Harder than it ever has before. Mine, too, is beating heavily. They are perfectly in sync.

Out of nowhere, he swoops down and pulls me up against him. I shriek, but wrap my arms around his neck. He's smiling his big, toothy smile. The blue of his eyes is soft and gentle. He leans forward until our noses brush.

"My *lehti,* my love, my heart, I love you as well. I love you more than words will ever be able to explain."

He leans forward and presses a soft kiss to my mouth, and the floodgates open up. I'm sobbing almost uncontrollably as he continues to press gentle kisses all over my face and neck. I can't stop it.

"My *lehti,* pleased do not cry. I cannot stand it. I do not like you sad."

Below us, KJ releases a deep, long sigh.

"She isn't sad, *apha*. She's overcome." We both look down. KJ shakes his little head in a perfect imitation of his Aunt Shay as he fumbles with his block. "She's overcome."

* * *

BATI

"Is it gonna bite me?"

I smile and ruffle my hand over KJ's head before urging him forward.

"Your *apha* would never send you toward danger, *dahni*. Now go. This is the last challenge. We must be brave so that we can be successful."

KJ edges closer to the nerve cluster. I can smell his apprehension, as well as that coming from my *lehti*.

"He is in no danger, my *lehti*."

"I know. I can't help it. Mama instincts." Her eyes are pinned to KJ who is nearly upon the cluster with his hand outstretched. Tiani's heart beats quickly, and mine does with it.

KJ stops when he's almost in contact with one of the long, thin reeds and glances back at me. His face is a mask of indecision.

"It is okay, K. Touch it. Trust me, it will not be as scary as you imagine. Be brave."

KJ's little brow furrows in resolve and he turns back, pushing his fingers against the stalk before jumping back.

A low buzz emanates from the cluster. KJ runs to where I stand with his mother and ducks behind my legs. I put a comforting hand at his back.

"Watch."

The stalks in the cluster spring to life, bending from their stiff forms and waving gently in the air. A bright white light pulses at the base of each stalk and travels its length until it reaches the top. Once there, a bright spark erupts from the tip.

"Cool!" KJ's awed response follows the disappearance of his fear.

Beside me, Tiani snorts before covering her mouth with her hand. She smells mischievous.

"What is humorous, my *lehti*?"

Her mouth quirks to the side before she peeks around to check if KJ is paying attention.

"K, you must record the reaction before it subsides. Do it as I have shown you."

KJ steps from the protection of my leg and holds his wrist up, tapping his band and engaging the record function.

"Now, what is on your mind."

She smiles shyly. "I was just thinking that this kind of reminds me of something."

"What does this remind you of?" I ask even though I have some idea.

"You know, the whole pulsing, erupting tip…" She stares at me as if waiting for me to show my understanding.

"I do not know."

"You don't know what long, pulsing thing that erupts at the tip I could be thinking of." Her eyes narrow.

"I do not," I return, but I cannot stop the smile that pulls at my mouth. She strikes out and hits me lightly on the arm.

"Yes, you do. You butthead."

I pull her against me and nuzzle her sweet-smelling hair. I have not taken enough time to learn all of her scents and taste all of her sweet places. Now that she is mine and has accepted the *leht*, I am glad that I will have time to learn all of these things.

"Perhaps when we get back to the campsite, I can present what I believe you speak of, and you can inform me if I am correct."

She rolls her eyes, but arousal colors her scent. "Maybe."

"Perhaps we should put him in films. Kwarq was an actor for a time." I lean in to whisper to Tiani as we make our way back through the forest to the campsite. KJ insisted on walking. My *lehti* didn't want to let him, but I convinced her he would be fine. So far, my *dahni* is traversing the forest quite well. He moves with surety ahead of us, holding tight to his pack as I have shown him.

KJ was quite proud of himself after he completed his final task. He performed an impromptu victory dance with accompanying song. It was very creative and well done.

Tiani snorts. "He's extra enough for it."

"This word, 'extra.' It means expressive?"

Tiani laughs. "Yes, hun. You should really let Amina teach you Ebonics."

"You could teach me." I reach out for her hand, and she takes it, squeezing our palms together.

"Don't worry, babe. I got you."

"Whoa, it's shakin!" We turn to KJ. He's stopped several feet ahead of us. His arms fan out as he wobbles his body back and forth in an exaggerated motion. A second later, the ground beneath my feet gives a rough tremble.

"That's new," Tiani mumbles, looking down. The surface of the mud quivers. After a moment, the trembling stops.

We all pause, waiting to see if anything further happens, and as if on cue, a geyser of water shoots out from the mud a few feet away. A second later, another erupts right beside Tiani. She yelps and jumps to the side as more and more jets of water spring up from the mud. The thick water quickly begins to lap around our ankles, and my heart lurches.

"Fountain!" KJ splashes through the water of a nearby spring. While a part of me wishes this was a moment for play, every one of my Lyqa instincts is warning of danger.

"We must return to the campsite."

I don't wait for Tiani to ask questions. I step forward and scoop KJ up and begin to move as quickly as I can through the forest.

Chapter 15

TIANI

Bati's gone quiet all of a sudden. He's carrying KJ again and booking it through the forest back in the direction of the campsite. His sudden change in demeanor has me a little shook.

"Is everything okay? You're acting like something is gonna jump out and eat us."

"There is nothing big enough to eat us, but there are other things."

"Uh, okay, but you said this was a safe *ta'ani*majig."

"I believed it to be relatively safe, but I was considering the danger from a Lyqa perspective. We are faster. Our senses are sharper…We can swim," he tags on at the end like he hates to say it. "For humans, especially a small child, this perhaps was not the best idea. Qiton is safe, but it is also unpredictable."

The way he says unpredictable makes me skip to catch up.

"We'll be okay, though? I mean, do you think something is gonna happen?"

Bati stops abruptly and turns to look at me. He looks guilty.

"I did not do as much research as I should have for this

time of year on Qiton. The tremor we felt earlier is the signal of a tide shift."

"What does that mean?"

"It means, that the solstice high tide is coming in sooner than I anticipated, and we must hurry to make it back to the campsite before the waters are too high."

Our heart beats fast. He's nervous. When he turns and continues rushing through the tall reeds, I follow, moving as quickly as I can.

By the time we get to the edge of the forest, the water is already lapping around my calves. The campsite is a tiny dot in the distance. I'm not so great with telling distances, but we have a mile, perhaps more before we get there.

"Do you think we'll make it?" I huff out.

Bati doesn't slow his steps. I'm jogging to keep up, and while I'm not completely inactive in my daily life back on Earth, I'm not a regular exerciser. I'm certainly not trek across alien terrain fit. The pace Bati's set has me a bit winded.

"We will make it, *lehti*," he replies but there's even more concern on his face.

I'm lagging. It's like I'm walking through cement. I look down. The water's nearly to my knees. When did that happen?

"Do not stop walking, *lehti*."

"The water is getting really high, Bati."

"I know, *lehti*."

My legs burn something fierce. This water is different. It's thicker. Less like water and more like a gel. I reach down and pull the hem of my Qitoni skirt all the way up to my waist. Modesty isn't something I give a shit about right now.

Freeing up my legs makes it a little easier to walk, but all the effort I've put in until now has worn me down. I'm struggling, and the little dot that's the campsite isn't getting any closer.

"Do we have far to go?"

Bati sighs, and it's the first time I've ever sensed impatience from him. I hate to be that *are we there yet* companion, but any idea that we are getting closer gives me the energy to continue.

"*Lehti,* we will make it."

He doesn't sound so sure.

BATI

I tell Tiani we will make it because I cannot think of any other truth. I cannot think that the waters will get too high before we have to swim. I cannot think it.

My *lehti* smells worried. I try to project some reassurance, but my own heart is beating faster than I can manage.

The water has been rising at a steady pace. Even with the unexpected change in conditions, high tide is coming in quicker than I anticipated. In the distance, I can just make out the campsite. I don't have to check my band to know that it's further than it should be. The fear that we will not make it, a fear that I've been trying to overcome, begins to take over. I push it away again and quicken my steps.

"We must hurry, *lehti,*" I tell her again.

I start to jog. The thick water makes movement slightly more difficult, but not as hard as it is for my *lehti.* Tiani is forced to run at my side. Her breath huffs out in painful bursts. She's not doing well. I can sense the ache in her body. The tension. I can also sense her determination. She's doing her best to keep up. She will continue as long as she can, and I comfort myself with the knowledge that my *lehti* is a fighter. I steady my heart to regulate our energy, and I keep the pace I have set. It is the only way.

* * *

Ten minutes later, the truth that I'm ignoring, that I cannot even allow to form in my mind, becomes too obvious to ignore. My *lehti* is tired and the water has gotten too high. I look down at her. Her face is set. She is so beautiful. Fear and sadness grip me.

"My *lehti,*" I force the words out. She looks up. Despite her fatigue, there is a smile ready for me. "The water is rising too quickly."

"We're too far?" I can barely make my muscles move to nod my head. She's quiet for a long moment. Her anxiety is tangy in my nostrils. "And there is nowhere to go? No place where I'll be safe?"

"There is not, but we will not give up. We will continue forward until we cannot, and then I will think of something. I will not leave you, *lehti.*"

"I mean, you might have to."

"*Lehti—*"

"*Dahni,*" she interjects. "We have a kid, Bati. I mean, he's yours, right? You love him like he's yours?"

"He is not like mine. He is mine."

"Good. So, if you have to choose, you choose him. We shouldn't even be in this situation. I should know how to swim. And if we can't make it in time, you're going to make sure KJ is safe, and that's it."

I can only stare at her. When I take too long to answer, anger flares in her scent.

"Right? Bati, say you'll choose him no matter what!"

I blink. Something warm and wet slides down my cheek. "I will, my *lehti.*"

She nods and swallows hard. I can detect the moisture in her eyes. I can smell the salt of her tears.

"Good, now let's keep moving. I don't want to drown, but I just want it to be clear that you're gonna look out for him."

"I will let nothing happen to him."

* * *

"Mommy's too far away." KJ's worried voice snaps me out of my head. I turn. Tiani is several paces away.

"Tiani—" I call to her. She shakes her head, as if she knows I am considering turning back, and waves her hands.

"I'm okay, Bati. Just keep going."

The water is at my waist. Tiani struggles against the nearly chest high sea level. Every part of me wants to go back for her. To find some way to keep us together for as long as possible. Suddenly, a thought occurs to me, and I turn, pushing through the water until I reach her. Her eyes are closed. Her fatigue is so great that I'm shocked she hasn't succumbed to it. Her eyes spring open when she hears me moving through the water.

"What the hell, Bati. Keep going, please. I can't do this if I think you're worried about me."

I ignore her and lift KJ onto my shoulders before pulling her up against me.

"Wrap your legs around me."

"Bati, no. You're too tired for that. Just let me go as long as I can."

"I am made to protect you. My first heart will give me the strength. I will get us as close as I can."

She sighs but wraps her legs around my waist, securing her ankles at my back. Now that she is close, her exhaustion is pungent in my nose. She takes hold of KJ's hands and rests her head against my chest. I hold her close, pressing her to my body, and start moving through the water again. A deep, exhausted sigh explodes from her mouth.

"God, Bati, I never would have said anything, but I was so fucking tired."

I press my lips to her soft curls. "I know, my *lehti*."

Chapter 16

TIANI

"We are almost there, *lehti.*"

He's lying. I snuck a glance. The sea willow is definitely closer, but the water is higher too. Bati holds me as far up on his body as he can. He can't put me any higher or else I'm going to be on his shoulders with KJ. And the water is still rising.

"How you doing, kiddo?"

KJ looks down at me.

"I'm okay, mommy."

He's such a brave, smart boy. He knows we're in trouble, but he's being such a trooper. I resist the urge to look at him. I don't want him to see the fear that I know shows on my face. I'm having a hard enough time coming to terms with the fact that pretty soon, I'm going to have to make Bati leave me. I try to remember all the stuff he taught me about floating. I try to think calming thoughts. I tell myself to relax. I can't float if I'm not relaxed. I think about making love to Bati in the water. How good I'd felt after. How serene. I think about how happy I am that my weird ass sister fell in love with an alien with a fine ass twin brother, and how lucky I am that Bati loves me…and KJ. I know he will take care of him. He got hit by a truck for him.

"I'm going to say something and don't be mad, okay?"

He swallows, and I can hear his throat working. "I will never be mad at you, my *lehti.*"

"I want you to keep KJ on Lyqa. I want him to stay with you. He loves you." I clear my throat because the sorrow is real. Our hearts are beating fast, and I try my best to breathe slowly. I can't float if I'm not calm. "I'm not going to panic, Bati. I'm going to try my best to stay calm. But if I can't do it, if you can't make it back to me in time, tell my mother and my sisters that I love them."

"I will, my *lehti.*" His voice is thick. I stare at the water. I can't look up.

"And, Bati?"

"Yes, Tee."

"You're the best thing that ever happened to me, and I love you. I love you so so much."

BATI

Tiani weeps quietly against my chest. She's holding tight to me, trying to keep the water from covering her mouth. I, too, stretch my neck as far above the water line as I can. I've been taking slow, deep breaths for several minutes. Our hearts keep a steady, easy beat. It is all I can do to stay calm. To prepare her for what we must do.

"Try to relax, Tiani."

She nods and swallows her next sob before sucking in a deep breath and pushing it out loudly.

"I just had to get it out, so I can focus."

"I understand."

"KJ, look at me." Tiani directs her attention above my head.

"Yes, mommy?" KJ's shaky voice sounds out near my ear.

"Your *apha* is going to take you to the campsite, okay? I'm going to stay here and practice my floating. Once he drops you off, he's going to come back and get me." Tiani's voice is easy. She is a good mother. The feeling that I have failed her is intense even as I know there was no way to foresee this.

"What if you go under water?"

"I won't go under water, baby. I'm gonna take shadow breaths."

"It's shallow breaths," KJ returns with a weak chuckle.

"That's right, baby. I'm gonna take shallow breaths."

Tiani turns back to me. Her gaze is shifty and nervous, but she smiles before leaning into kiss me. I sweep into her mouth when she opens for me, tasting as much of her as I can. She pushes against my shoulders to end the kiss even as I lean in for more.

"I will come back for you. I will not let you drown."

"I know."

We both look in the direction of the sea willow. It's close, but not close enough. With my speed, it will still take about fifteen minutes to get there and back. Fifteen minutes. I send a plea to the universe that Tiani can stay afloat that long.

"We should discard our packs. KJ can keep his." I ease first one strap then the other off my shoulders and let my pack go.

"There's nothing important in there?" Tiani's eyes follow the pack as it drifts across the water.

An instinctual need to protect flares fiercely through me. "I am holding the only important things in my life."

Her mouth curves up into a sad smile. "Set me up?"

I help her remove her pack and the cumbersome Qitoni garb so it's easier for her to float.

"What about your stuff?" KJ protests as the packs float way.

"Mommy's going to watch our stuff, baby. Don't worry,"

Tiani reassures him.

I don't waste any more time. I push Tiani away. She relaxes her body and leans back as I brace her beneath the back and legs until she's level in the water.

"Just breathe, *lehti*. I will be back. Whatever happens, just breathe."

"Let's have some babies."

I blink. "*Lehti*?"

"If I make it, let's have some babies. I love you. Let's just do it all."

I try to smile, but the pain in my chest is too great. "Once I come for you and get you to safety, I will give you as many babies as you want."

"Okay. I'm gonna think about our babies. That will keep me calm."

I hold her until the water carries her weight, and then I let her go. She drifts a little. Her eyes are closed. Her chest rises and falls above the water.

"You are doing well, Tiani. I will be back before you know it."

I lift KJ from my shoulders and bring him around to my front.

"I'm going to hold you in front of me, *dahni*. Kick your legs as long as you can."

KJ's chin wobbles. The water is colder than expected. The sun has started to set, and without her clothes, Tiani is in even greater danger of being affected by the elements.

"What about mommy?"

I look back. Tiani is still floating a few feet away. I meet KJ's worried gaze and chuck him beneath the chin.

"Your *amha* will be fine. I am coming right back for her."

"We're gonna come back for you mommy!" he shouts across the water.

"I know, baby." Tiani's voice is calm, but I know this will

not last for long.

I push us off. KJ's little legs kick out beside me. Our process is not as fast as Lyqa speed, but it is quick. The sea willow gets closer. KJ's breath puffs out beside me.

"We are almost there, *dahni.*"

We've been swimming for nearly ten minutes when I reach out and grab the base of the sea willow. My arms shake as I lift KJ onto the first step above water.

"Run to the top, my *dahni,* and do not come back down. Not at all. Even if we take a long time to return. If we are not here by nighttime, use the blanket in your pack to stay warm and then tap your band and say, 'call Uncle Ah'dan,' okay?"

He stares down at me, shivering on the step.

"Tell me what I have said."

"Don't leave. Use my blanket if I get cold, and in the nighttime, if you and mommy aren't here, call Uncle Ah'dan."

"Good. You are such a smart, special boy, KJ. Your *apha* loves you."

"I love you, too."

I only stay long enough to see him turn and run up the side of the sea willow before I start swimming away. My arms burn with the effort to push myself through the thick water, but I persist. I gather every bit of strength I have, willing my first heart to do what it is made for, and I head back in the direction I have left my *lehti.*

After a while, I know I have been swimming for too long. A low fog has settled over the water, obstructing my view somewhat, but I know I have not gone the wrong way. I paid attention to every shift in direction. I am grateful in this way for my Lyqa senses, and I am more scared than ever because I should have come upon her already. I stop and tread water, turning around in a circle.

"Tiani?" I keep my voice even out of fear that I may startle her out of her float. Silence surrounds me. The only sound is the gentle lap of the sea.

"*Lehti*!" I cannot stop the panic that fills me. I push off again, swimming for a few seconds. Perhaps she has drifted further than I anticipated. "Tiani?"

Again, I am met with nothing but silence. A few feet away, something floats. I hurry toward it, but my relief is dashed when I see that it is just my pack. I was not incorrect. This is where I left her. Except, she is not here.

And then I feel it—tug in my chest, the feeling of constraint. My heart thumps an off-kilter rhythm, like it's trying to beat as some outside force attempts to stop it. The moment I feel it, I know she has gone under and is somewhere out here dying.

TIANI

I dropped my damn butt.

I was doing really well before the fog showed up. I could feel myself drifting with the slow rock of the water, but I tried to stay calm. I told myself that even if I floated a bit away, Bati would find me. Then something brushed my leg, and I panicked, thinking it was a giant fish or worse, and dropped my butt.

I flail around in the water, trying my best to do cupcake hands, but only managing to tire myself out and swallow water. Too soon, the last of my energy drains and I start to sink.

.

.

.

"He is looking for you, little one."

Sol's voice has that same robotic quality in my head. I'm

moving slowly through the water. I tried to hold my breath for as long as I could, but my chest started to burn and it was like my mouth opened on its own. Air has been leaking slowly from between my lips, and with each breath I release, I sink a little more.

It's so quiet. I feel like I've been sinking forever. I know I'm not dead yet, but I can sense it creeping at the corners of my mind. All I can think about is KJ and Bati and my mother. Amina's face flashes through my mind. That stupid little dance she did when I said I would come to Lyqa. I should be pissed about agreeing, but I can't be. Because Bati. And Bati.

"He is looking for you."

"I know, Sol. Tell him to go back."

I bit more air escapes my mouth and I drop a little lower. My heart thumps heavily in my chest. Every beat takes so long to happen that I wonder I'm still alive.

Again, I think of KJ and Bati and my mother. I think of Kwarq's big toothy smile. Ah'dan's easy grin. I think of LaShay. So weird. So sincere. She really is a good aunt.

"Who is that woman?" Sol's voice is sharp in my head. It sounds—different.

"Shay."

"Who is Sheh?" I inside laugh at his pronunciation.

"My sister."

"Where is she?"

"On Lyqa. Did you tell him to go back?"

"I will not go back. Where are you, my lehti*?"*

Bati's voice cuts in and my heart thumps.

"I don't know. I went down."

"I am looking for you."

"I love you, Bati. Go back."

"I love you, too, my lehti. *Do you have any breath?"*

"A little."

"Then call me. Nice and loud, so I can hear you."

I feel for the small hint of breath that's left in me. It's just a whisper, so slight that I can't really get hold of it, but I do. I hold it and gather it, and then I open my mouth, and I scream.

Chapter 17

BATI

Tiani begins to cough and spit up the dark sea water the moment we break the surface. My ears are still ringing. Her piercing scream sounded out so loudly in the water that I had no trouble locating her. Although, I'd gotten to her just in time. The delay between the beat of our hearts had become too long. Any longer and I would have lost her, but this is not something I will allow myself to think of.

"I have you. You are okay, my *lehti*."

"I dropped my damn butt."

I chuckle despite the intense terror that gripped me a moment ago and paddle us over to Sol's hovering craft.

"You did very well, my *lehti*. You had not been under for long, and I would never have let you drown."

Sol opens the panel as we approach, and KJ's head springs out from the interior.

"Mommy!"

Tiani reaches for Sol who hauls her out of the water and into the craft with little effort. Immediately, she pulls our *dahni* against her, sobbing over him. I pull myself up beside them, sliding the craft door closed. My body is tired, but it does not stop me from pulling both my *lehti* and *dahni* onto my lap. I only want to have them close. KJ holds tight to his mother, and she smooths her hand over his back in comfort.

"I'm sorry I scared you, baby."

"I wasn't scared, mommy. I knew *apha* would find you. He swimmed so fast!"

Tiani reaches a hand up to cradle my face, and when I look down, her eyes shine with fresh tears.

"Swam, baby. He swam so fast."

"Does that feel good?"

I groan as Tiani kneads her hands into the muscles of my back. My body aches from my efforts on Qiton.

We have only been home for a short while. The entire family was anxious to hear the dramatic events of our trip, especially when KJ began relaying details the moment we stepped in the house, but I'd managed to carry my *lehti* to our apartments where I can have her to myself. I need time to stare at her, to assure myself she is well. Although, she has been taking care of me since when got to our room.

"Oh, my *lehti*. This is the best thing I have ever felt in my life. What is it called?"

She chuckles. "A massage."

"And this is done as a service to partners?"

"It can be, but it is also something that you can pay someone to do for you."

I flip over Lyqa fast and pull her over my hips to straddle me.

"Do not pay anyone to do this service for you. I will do it for free," I tell her.

She resumes her movements over my aching pecs.

"So that shot I got. It's just going to cancel out my birth control?" She leans down to press a soft kiss to my chest and my cock stiffens.

"It will return you to a fertile state, yes." I brought her to a healing center the moment we returned to Lyqa. While there, she inquired about reversing her conception prevention, and was given a shot to neutralize the hormones she has been taking.

"Good," she murmurs as she leans down to press a kiss to my lips. When she straightens above me again, I take the time to look at her. My eyes roam over her beautiful brown face. The sharp curves of her cheekbones. The full, lushness of her lips. I am grateful every second that she is with me and loves me and knows that I love her.

"You got an eyesight problem?"

As she speaks, she rises up and reaches between us to release my cock from my sleeping shorts. She nudges aside her undergarments and lowers herself onto me. A harsh groan rumbles in my chest as her tight, warmth settles over me.

"Ah, my *lehti*. If this means that I can think of no greater sight than that of my *lehti*, my heart, and my love. Then yes, I am afflicted with such an ailment."

TIANI

"Oh my god, this is horrible!"

I lean back over the toilet and heave again. I don't know how it's possible that I'm still puking. There's nothing left in my stomach, even though it feels really tight and full. Like I drank a gallon of water.

"It is the conception sickness, *lehti*. It will pass."

Bati strokes my back, but that doesn't stop me from lifting my head to glare at him.

"You did *not* tell me this was going to happen." I barely get the words out before my stomach jerks again, and I have to turn back to the toilet. This is so gross. I didn't have one day of morning sickness with KJ. Not one.

Bati chuckles, and I could punch him.

"Would it have stopped you from climbing on top of me if I had?"

I shoot him another look and it only makes him chuckle again.

"Do not be upset with me *lehti*. I have only done what you asked and given you babies."

My head jerks up again. "Babies?"

He shrugs. "It is likely. Twins of my kind will almost always produce twins. It was this way with my brother and your sister."

I roll my eyes and stick my head back into the toilet. The next two months can't be over quick enough.

"Aw!" I want to cry, and I don't even know why. I'm going to assume it's the Lyqa hormones. I know what Amina meant now. The urge to weep is like a thing crawling through me.

I bend over the bed where Amina cradles her son and daughter. They peer up at her, wiggling in their swaddles. Amina murmurs softly to them, and they settle.

Their little faces come into view.

I blink.

I look at Bati who's smiling down at his nephew and niece. No one else seems alarmed by the fact that Amina's kids look nothing like either her or Kwarq.

I turn my back to Amina and nudge Bati in the side. He grunts when my elbow connects sharply with his ribs.

"So, we're all just gonna pretend her kids don't look just like you? You got something you want to tell me, dude?" I know it's stupid, but I'm like for real mad.

Behind me, Amina cackles loudly, startling the babies and making them fuss. Kwarq lifts his daughter from her arms. LaShay takes our nephew and rocks away with him, cooing and pressing kisses to his round, little blue-black face. KJ follows, straining his neck to get a glimpse of the baby.

"Oh, you didn't know? Me and Bati totally got it on when I was here before. It's a Lyqa thing." Amina shakes her head at me and gives an exaggerated eye roll. "Jesus, Tee. No one did your man, girl. Apparently, Lyqa genes are like the lottery. Who knows what your kids are going to look like."

I turn to Bati to find him looking at me with an amused expression.

"You know I had not joined with anyone when I met you," he says without an ounce of shame. Amina sucks her teeth and I turn to find her giving Kwarq the side eye.

"Mm, how come you weren't a virgin when I met you?"

Kwarq spares my sister the barest glance before discreetly rolling his eyes to the side.

"You are the only woman of my heart. Do not worry about what came before you. You are all that is."

Damn. I raise an impressed eyebrow at Amina and her mouth curves into a wide smile.

"I better be."

"You are."

I turn to Bati.

"Ahem."

He stares blankly at me. "What would you have me say that I have not already?"

"I don't know. Some mushy shit like that." I turn away, inexplicably salty. It rushes over me. These Lyqa hormones are no joke.

A second after my back is turned, Amina gasps. Her hand comes up to cover her mouth, and tears immediately fill her eyes.

"What—" I turn. Bati is on his knee. He holds a small open box between us. Inside, on a pillow of fabric, is a silver ring with a large, bright blue diamond in the middle. At least I think it's a diamond. It doesn't look like any stone I've ever seen, but it catches the light and reflects every color of the rainbow. It reminds me of the sky the first night we came to Lyqa.

Bati smiles up at me, and there is no denying the love shining in his own bright blue eyes.

"Is 'Marry me' sufficiently mushy shit?"

I burst into tears, throwing myself at him so we fall back to the floor as I press kisses all over his face. From somewhere in the quiet of the room, KJ's little voice sounds out.

"Ooo, *apha*, you cursed."

The End.

Say It Like A Lyqa

- Kwarq : KwahR-q (Hard R, Q is a click in the throat)
- Bati : Pah-tee
- Ah'dan : Ah-Dahn (breathy H both times with a noticeable pause between syllables)
- Quth : Kooth (K is a soft click in the throat)
- Mahdi : Makh-Di (H is a little harsh)
- Li'aht : Lee-aut
- T'nai : Teh-Nye
- Maq'ti : Mock-Tee (CK is soft click in the throat)
- Qim : Keem (K is a soft click in the throat)
- Qiton : Kee-tahn
- S'wad : Soo-Wad
- Qitoni : Kee-tah-ni
- Soluanitiat'ti Somiiti'un : So-lu-ah-ni-ti-ah-ti Soh-my-ti-oon
- Somii - Soh-my